I0573795

A Taste of Honey

Iris Leach

CRIMSON
ROMANCE
F+W Media, Inc.

Published by
Crimson Romance
an imprint of F+W Media, Inc.
10151 Carver Road, Suite 200
Blue Ash, Ohio 45242

www.crimsonromance.com

Copyright © 2012 by Iris Leach

ISBN 10: 1-4405-6054-4
ISBN 13: 978-1-4405-6054-5
eISBN 10: 1-4405-6055-2
eISBN 13: 978-1-4405-6055-2

This is a work of fiction. Names, characters, corporations, institutions, organizations, events, or locales in this novel are either the product of the author's imagination or, if real, used fictitiously. The resemblance of any character to actual persons (living or dead) is entirely coincidental.

Dedication

Michael. Thanks for all your support and love.
I know I drive you crazy at times.

Chapter One

Courtship is a lost art.

"Are you okay, Charli? It's a shock, but I didn't know how else to tell you."

Judy Jenkins' voice bit into the sad confusion of her mind. "When did it happen?"

"Last night."

She clenched her bottom lip. This was so sad. Grief tore at Charli's heart. "Poor Mr. Knight. How did he—did he suffer?"

"His ticker gave out. He died in his sleep. He didn't feel a thing, Charli. Just didn't wake up, that's all." Judy came around her desk and gave her a warm hug. "Are you okay? You're such a softie."

She nodded. A thick knot caught somewhere in Charli's throat. She couldn't swallow. She was going to cry. She just knew she was. It was the shock. One moment she was joking and talking to Mr. Knight and the next he was gone. It was such an unreal sensation.

She looked over at his office door as if expecting him to poke around his head and say, "Any coffee, Charli?" Knowing full well she always had coffee percolating and iced buns in the stationery cupboard, a particular favorite of his.

"Was he alone?"

Judy gave a wry smile. "Only you'd ask that question, Charli. He was in bed and since I don't think Mr. Knight had any love interest since his wife died, he was alone."

She pulled herself erect. "Judy, you know what I meant. Was he alone in the house?"

"Yes, he was alone. His housekeeper found him this morning."

She'd been so fond of Mr. Knight, and now she'd never see him again. It was too awful to bear. "He said he didn't feel well. He complained of pain in the chest. I told him to go home and rest, but he wouldn't. He said he'd be all right." She ran her fingertips lightly across her brow. "I should have insisted."

"Now don't go and blame yourself. You couldn't have known how ill he really was. Anyway he was bull-headed and always did exactly what he wanted."

Tears dripped down her face. "He was a very private person." She groped into her desk drawer for a box of tissues. Plucking one, she blew her nose loudly. "He always had time to listen to my woes."

"He took a special interest in you; protective, like a dad would be, and he wouldn't have a word said against you, no way."

Charli smiled at the memory. Mr. Knight was considerate toward her. His greatest desire was to see her married to a nice man who'd look after her. He believed in the sanctity of marriage. The blessed union of one man and one woman until *death do us part*.

Get married, Charli, he'd said. It's the only way to a contented life. And she'd smile and say she hadn't met Mr. Right.

She was old-fashioned in her outlook on romance. She wanted to be courted like her father had courted her mother. She'd loved hearing the tales her mother told her about how her father had taken her out to dinner, bringing her chocolate and flowers. They picnicked at the beach and danced to a blues jazz band at the local dancehall. He wooed her until she fell in love with him, and he'd finally proposed and she'd gladly accepted. So romantic.

She didn't expect a knight in shining armor on a white steed sort of thing, but a man who knew how to court a woman. How to make her feel special, assuring her that he'd do anything for her that was within his power.

"His work was his life." Her eyes flew to Judy's. "His work? What will become of the business now?"

"There's a nephew, William Knight. I've heard he's coming to take over the reins."

"Does he know anything about publishing?"

"He runs a small publishing house in Darwin."

Surprised, she said, "I didn't know anything about that. Mr. Knight didn't mention he even had a nephew."

Judy was the office receptionist, and besides the fact that she'd been working here for years, what she didn't know about everyone in the office wasn't worth knowing. Mr. Knight always said that Judy had radar implanted in her brain. It focused in on all the office gossip. It wasn't that Judy was malicious; to the contrary, she had a warm and giving heart. She was a natural born sticky-beak and loved to know everybody's business.

"Don't suppose he wanted to talk about it. The family was in shock for years."

"Shock? What were they shocked about?"

"Over what happened to his nephew."

Had William Knight taken a car on a joy ride in his youth? Or maybe tax evasion or failing to stop at a red light. "Something bad happened to his nephew?"

"Too bloody right it did."

Her interest piqued. Charli leant forward and said, "Don't leave out a thing, Judy. Tell me all."

"Young Mr. Knight fell in love with his chief editor. They married, and a few years later, she ran off with his star author, taking half of his most popular writers with her. She started up her own business here in Melbourne. Might have heard of it. Powerful Press."

"Yes, I have." Charli loved gossip. What woman didn't? "Tell me more."

"Nothing more to tell. Young Mr. Knight struggled to keep his business afloat, and through hard decision-making and sheer business brilliance managed to do so."

"This is so unbelievably juicy," she said.

"He should have sued the pants off her."

"Don't be so pedantic, Judy. She was a witch with a capital B." Charli placed a hand over her heart and said, "She broke his heart. Our Young Mr. Knight is sensitive and obviously very romantic."

Would William Knight be a younger version of his uncle, short, slightly overweight, balding? Well, perhaps not balding, but hair receding slightly at the temples and forehead; a friendly man with a boisterous laugh and generous disposition who would visit the office twice, three times a week, just to keep his finger in the pie.

A beautiful vision came into her mind. *Miss Honey, I need to express myself with my art and wish to lock myself in a turret and paint. So therefore I'm giving you a promotion and putting you in charge of running Knight Books. You are more than capable.*

A surge of excitement. This was her big opportunity, she just knew it.

"Ah, well, not my business." Judy contradicted and Charli hid a smile. "Wanna do lunch?"

"That'd be great."

"See you at one."

Charli walked to her office window; the day was wet and windy as only Melbourne could be in May. She gazed out on to the multistory buildings. Everything must be perfect for the new boss. She would impress him with her professionalism; her efficiency; and, if he chose to stay at the helm, become his reliable right-hand.

In her mind's eye she saw herself standing side-by-side with young Mr. Knight. They were staring off into the not-too-distant future. The wind was blowing through her hair, a look of grim determination on her face and his arm draped around her shoulders. No, no, too intimate. Shoulder to shoulder. Sort of like Leonardo DiCaprio and Kate Winslet in Titanic standing at the helm, or was it starboard? Their love much stronger than their fear of death. So romantic, she'd seen the movie four times.

Sighing deeply, she returned to her desk and made notes on a pad. Leaning back in her chair, she tapped her lower teeth with the end of a pen. Number one, she had to sort through Mr. Knight's papers, and he wasn't the tidiest of men, bluntly refusing to let her organize his desk when her hands were itching to do so.

There was a lot to do before his nephew arrived.

Would he, as she hoped, pass the running of Knight Books on to her, or would he have completely different ideas from his uncle on how to run the company? Either way, she could cope. She was a professional and knew the ropes. He would have to read her work reports and know how proficient she was and how she was an asset to Knight Books.

She threw the pen onto her desk. "Time will tell," she said aloud. "Time will tell."

*

William Knight sighed. He hadn't quite come to terms with the loss of his uncle. Now it was only his mother and him. It hadn't been easy, but he'd come to a decision. Leave Darwin in the capable hands of Stan McFee and take up the reins of Knight Books. He could think of no alternative.

Going back to Melbourne struck his quivering nerves like a snapped guitar string. He pushed his thumbs into the pits of his eyes and cursed softly. Darwin not being big enough for the two of them, Mavis's words not his, she'd scurried off to Melbourne with Brad Wilde, his top writer, clinging to her side. She'd betrayed him both personally and professionally.

He'd fallen for Mavis's dark beauty hook, line, and sinker. Taught her the ropes of running a publishing house, and, without warning, she'd started her own business and taken every worthwhile author she could with her. Charmed and armed, that was Mavis. Planned every move she'd ever made.

There'd be no escaping running into her at some time or another in Melbourne. How would he handle that ugly situation? Smile and a handshake, or snarl and turn his back?

Her stabbing him in the back didn't happen immediately. It took years of clever planning, learning the ropes, ingratiating herself with everybody. Hell, even the cleaner loved Mavis and lit up like a Christmas tree every time she spoke to him. Come to think of it, he went with her too.

If she never gave him anything else, she'd given him a deep mistrust of women in business. He'd never work hand-in-glove with a woman again. He didn't trust their soft smiles. The enticing lure that lay deep in their baby blues like a dangling worm to an unsuspecting fish. He'd learned a hard lesson and he'd learned it well.

He looked up as Stan McFee ambled into his office. He liked Stan very much and they'd become firm friends over the years. Often he had dinner with Stan and his wife, Lauren, a beautiful ex-model that men gave prolonged lustful looks. Will knew her as a woman whose life revolved around her family's happiness. When they'd made Lauren, they had thrown away the mold. "All set to go, Will?"

"Yeah. Ready but not quite willing. Think you can handle things here, Stan?"

"You've asked me that question a hundred times."

"Sorry."

"That's okay." He flung his long frame into a chair, stretching out his legs in front of him. "So you know who you'll be working with?"

"Charles Honey. And by all accounts, he's one capable chief editor." He glanced at Honey's work reports. "Funny thing, Stan. He's only temporary in the position. My uncle never made him permanent chief editor. No worries. I'll tidy that up quick smart."

"So all your worries were for nothing?"

"It's made me feel easier having a man working with me. I couldn't take a woman, Stan. No way. I'd go nuts."

Stan laughed. "Your reputation laughs at your denial, Will. You're a woman's man from way back."

"I'm not talking about my private life. You know what I mean."

"Not every woman in business is like your ex."

"I have no qualms about women in business, what I don't want is a woman working side by side with me. Now I won't have to face that. Thank God for Charles Honey."

Will pushed himself back in his chair. It wouldn't be so bad. Running Knight Books was the challenge he needed. He was getting soft here in Darwin. Back in the big time was called for. Charles Honey was a top man. Yeah, things were going to be okay.

*

Charli had hoped she'd meet young Mr. Knight at the funeral. As it turned out it was only a small service in the chapel with sandwiches and coffee later. She'd asked around but it had appeared that young Mr. Knight had left immediately after the service. She consoled herself she'd meet him soon enough.

No sooner than she'd thought that, a fax arrived stating that William Knight would be arriving at the office early the next day.

Charli had Malcolm Knight's office thoroughly cleaned in preparation for William Knight's arrival. She moved into his office and glanced around. Maybe she should get some flowers as a welcome from the staff. She buzzed the intercom. "Yes, Charli?"

"Judy, order some long-stemmed yellow roses and irises to be delivered first thing in the morning—no, have them delivered now. You never know, our young Mr. Knight may get here sooner than he said."

"Sure thing, Charli."

"And, Judy."

"Yes?"

"Don't stint on them. We want Mr. Knight to feel very welcome for his first day with us."

She studied the desk once more, everything in its place and a place for everything. She moved the telephone a fraction toward the edge of the desk, bringing his desk lamp a little further toward his chair.

Hands on her hips, she said aloud, "I think our young Mr. Knight should be content with his office. I can't wait to meet you, William Knight. If you're half as nice as your uncle then we should have a good working relationship."

Chapter Two

Courtship was far more interesting in the caveman era.

Will had decided to stay at his uncle's house rather than the hotel he always stayed at when in Melbourne. The house was old but comfortable and only six kilometers from the Central Business District. His mother lived too far out of the city to argue that he should stay with her. Thank God. He loved his mother dearly but she drove him crazy. What his mother needed, he'd decided, was the love of a good man. She'd been too long on her own and at forty-nine too young to remain a widow.

He'd left the funeral directly after the service. Although anxious to meet everyone, and especially Charles Honey, Will thought it was neither the time nor place to meet the staff and discuss the future of Knight Books. He'd get into work early tomorrow. Fresh and vital, he'd interview each staff member personally. Well, he'd have Charles beside him advising him all the way.

Moving to the sideboard, he poured himself a generous splash of Johnny Walker. Excited now about taking over the reins, he sipped the fiery liquid, his mind brimming with ideas about expanding the business, and if Charles Honey was as good as his record stated, then he was the man who could help him make Knight Books the best publishing house in Australia.

He wouldn't bombard Charles with new ideas too soon as he wasn't sure what type of man he was dealing with. He may be sensitive about change, or he may be a man who grabbed new innovations in two hands and went along with all Will's suggestions. Will hoped for the latter.

As soon as they could, they'd have a chin wag about what to do, which way to go. Will wanted to talk to each staff member, assure them that their jobs were safe. All he expected was loyalty and a fair day's work for a fair day's pay. His uncle had stuck firmly to traditional publishing but Will had ideas about going into e-pub, especially with fiction. It was the way of the future.

Will squashed himself into a large sofa and took a swallow of the whiskey. He nestled himself deeper into the soft leather and gazed at a rather pompous painting of his uncle hanging over the fireplace. His aunt had had it commissioned for his uncle's sixtieth birthday. It reminded Will of the Lord of the Manor surveying his estate and manor house. His uncle was nothing like that at all. He'd been a kind and generous man who always helped someone in trouble. His staff had loved him unconditionally because of his fairness and sense of trust he'd placed in everyone he met.

His uncle had always been there for him. Guiding him, advising him, encouraging him when he wanted to buy the run-down publishing house in Darwin. Applauding him when he'd succeeded in making it one of the most respected houses in Darwin. He loved his uncle very much and tried to model himself on him.

Raising his glass to the painting, Will said, "Here's to you, Uncle. I promise that I'll make Knight Books the best publishing house I can."

It'd take a while to settle down and it wouldn't be easy taking his uncle's place. Staff usually didn't like change, forced or otherwise. But he also knew that he could win their trust and loyalty once he proved to them that he was the same cut as his uncle.

The only true downer he could think of was that his mother would want him to meet every single girl she could find. Okay, he could live with that. He liked women's company. Just because he'd been hurt and humiliated didn't mean his urges had died. But he was careful about his choice of woman. If they started cooking him lamb roast and apple pies or wanted to take his dirty laundry home wrapped in brown paper, he'd back off.

He knew his mother wanted him married and she wanted grandkids. He felt a tug of compassion that this was something he could never give her, and somehow he had to make her understand that he'd never marry again. Once hurt, a million times shy.

He finished off the whiskey, rose from the chair and walked to the large French doors and out onto a beautiful stone veranda overlooking a magnificent garden.

He'd take over the reins tomorrow. All a man needed was a challenge to get the blood surging through his veins.

Maybe Charles could arrange a cocktail party where he could meet the authors. Maybe he should take the staff out for lunch to get to know them in a more relaxed atmosphere and vice versa.

There was so much to learn, and so many people to meet that Will gave a silent prayer of thanks for Charles Honey. A man he could rely on. A man he could trust not to stab him in the back.

The first thing he'd do was to make Charles' job permanent. He didn't want to lose him, and, as an added incentive, give him a raise.

Yeah, man, life was great.

Chapter Three

Bring her candy and flowers.
Shower her with gifts and write her a love-letter.

Charli had made sure she arrived early for work, but she still hadn't arrived before the young Mr. Knight as she could hear him moving about in his office. She hesitated outside his office door, her hand raised as if to knock. She lowered her hand, moved away, and sat at her desk pondering on the correct course of action. She wanted to appear professional and in control of any situation. Show him that she handled any new circumstance that came her way with a clear head and strong shoulders. A chief editor he could rely on in any emergency.

She imagined he'd be uneasy, on edge about taking over the reins. After all, he knew no one here at the house. She'd be the calmness he was seeking, the friend in need, and the comrade-in-arms he could rely on.

Still, the question remained, should she barge in and introduce herself or wait until she was summoned? Her answer came to her with the sound of a buzz from the intercom. "Please, come into my office."

His voice had sounded firm but nice. Heart resolute and spine ramrod straight, she was nervous and excited at the same time. She straightened her skirt and fluffed her hair, taking a quick peep in the mirror to reassure herself that everything was in place for the big meeting. Drawing in a deep breath, she entered his office. A large hulk of a figure sat behind the desk.

"What in the hell—?" he said rising to his feet.

Charli was looking into the face of the most overpoweringly handsome man she'd ever seen in her life. His eyes had a hypnotic

16

effect. A gaze that was as fascinating as drifting leaves in an autumn's breeze. When William Knight walked into a room, women the world over liquefied. Her eyes lowered and, oh my God, his mouth. A vision of it pressed against hers filled Charli with the strangest and most wonderful sensation.

He stood and moved around the desk to stand in front of her. Charli, at five-foot-seven was dwarfed by the sheer height of the man facing her.

"Mr. Knight? I'm Charli Honey, Mr. Knight's chief editor—I mean the deceased Mr. Knight's chief editor—no, your chief editor."

She was going to blow his socks off with her professionalism, instead she'd lost every bit of decorum, her usual polish now dim and tarnished. She felt as inept and defenseless as a rabbit cowering before a dingo.

The green eyes weighed her up. "Sorry, I don't mean to appear rude, it's your name that threw me." He glanced down at some papers on his desk, tapping a sheet of paper with the end of his pen.

"My name?"

"I thought you were male. And that you're definitely not."

"What has me being male or female got to do with anything?"

What was with this man? He was talking in circles. There definitely was a communication barrier between them. Damn. That's so not what she wanted. She wanted them to be working mates from the word go. *Okay, okay, take it easy. Try to calm down. I'm nervous and that's only natural.* She took a deep yoga breath through her nostrils and thought of green forests and sweet baby does.

"Everything, Honey. I've just been reading your file. Very impressive."

The forest dissolved into hot desert and sandstorms as her feminist instincts stood up and yelled inequity. How dare he call her *honey*? She wasn't his honey! She was no one's honey. Still, she refrained from chastising him, for the moment at least. "Thanks. I hope you'll be satisfied with my work, Mr. Knight."

"I'm sure we can work things out."

Slightly taken aback at his words, she said, "Work things out? What do you mean?" The first warning that something was wrong snapped her brain as the long cruel hand of fear took her by the neck and shook her. Something wasn't quite kosher.

He sighed and raked his hand through his thick thatch of black hair. His gaze met hers. His eyes were so green. Deep penetrating green. She'd never seen a man with green eyes before. Hazel yes. Blue, brown, and gray but never green. They were incredible. This man might be insensitive about another's feelings, but he was dazzling.

She suddenly wished they could have met under different circumstances. She wished that he liked her and that this conversation wasn't taking place. She wished they'd met at a party.

His office dissolved...

I'm casually sipping a gin and tonic. William Knight walks in. Stunning in his tight jeans, white T-shirt and black Bomber jacket. Our eyes lock. Fascinated, he ambles to my side and wraps his arm around my waist. "Dance with me, you captivating wench," he breathes.

With a toss of my head, I throw the glass to the floor; laughing at my power over this man.

We dance like we're made for each other. He lowers his head and his sexy mouth finds mine in a kiss that explodes—

*

"Honey," Will said. He'd been having a one-way conversation for the last few minutes. Charli Honey, although one of the loveliest women he'd seen in a long time, was a little bit odd, to say the least. She was staring off into space as if she'd seen the landing of aliens.

She blinked. She swallowed. "Yes," she said.

"Do you have a hearing problem?"

"My hearing is perfect."

"It's like talking to a brick wall."

"My mind wandered, that's all."

"Is it back with us now?" He grinned.

"What were you saying, Mr. Knight?"

He tapped papers. "You're position as chief editor is temporary. The position has never been filled."

She eyeballed him. "Filled?"

Will had to admit he felt bad. He didn't like what he was doing, it didn't sit well with him. But the alternative? She might put Bathsheba to shame, but my God, no way. Anyway, hadn't David ended up murdering Bathsheba's husband? "You must understand that I can't allow this discrepancy to continue."

"—Discrepancy?"

"The position will be advertised in-house and in several major newspapers."

"Advertised?"

"You seem to be repeating me, Honey."

"That's because I'm trying to understand what's going on here."

"What don't you understand?"

"None of it."

Hell. He studied her lovely face, her glorious red hair that swung low over her shoulders, the warmth of her coffee-colored eyes, and wished they had met under different circumstances. He liked what he saw very much and that made it extremely dangerous for them to be working together. What if he fell for her? What if behind those fantastic eyes and that innocent expression was a schemer? My God, she could have the same plans as Mavis. His safe world trembled. Maybe she'd imagined now that his uncle had died that she'd be taking over the reins of Knight Books? She was too beautiful to be trusted.

"Your position as chief editor is temporary. My uncle never made it permanent. My hands are tied. This was never meant to be a temporary position. You must understand this."

"So where does this leave me?"

"You'll revert back to your former position as editor." *I'll make it worth her while. Same wages. A bonus for work well done.* He felt more at ease now. As if he was doing her a favor.

He saw fire in her eyes. "I've been doing the job for nearly a year."

"And admirably. Thanks for doing a great job." He wanted the interview over. "You can apply for the position the same as everyone."

"Gee, thanks. Who'll be doing the interviewing?"

"Me."

"So it'd be a waste of time, wouldn't it, Mr. Knight. I mean if you were interested in me as your CE then we wouldn't be having this conversation."

"It's not fair to the other employees who might like the CE's job. They, like you," he hastened to add, "want the chance to get it."

He left her to return to his chair. He picked up his pen and wrote furiously on a pad. He could feel her eyes burning into the top of his head. "Thanks, Honey. That'll be all for now." What could he do to alleviate the tension between them? His eyes fell on the crystal vase of flowers. He imagined Honey would have been responsible for placing them on his desk. Nice gesture.

*

Interview over.

Charli made her way to his office door. The realization of

what was happening descending like a wet blanket. Her anger turned to despair and a lump as big as a concrete block filled her throat. He was getting rid of her. A real don't-call-me-I'll-call-you type of bloke. All her wild fanciful suppositions suddenly held no comparison to the truth. This couldn't be Malcolm Knight's nephew. Surely none of Malcolm Knight's genes were in this man's body. William Knight's Y gene was definitely Y for yobbo, yokel and, and—she couldn't think of another Y word.

"Before you leave, Honey."

Hope flared as she turned to face him. He stared at her. Her legs weak under the spellbinding gaze of crushed emeralds. *Get a grip here, Charli, this guy is public enemy number one and he sees you as Dick Tracy.* "Yes, Mr. Knight?" she said eagerly.

"Thank whoever put the flowers in my office. It's a warm welcome."

"It was Judy. Your receptionist." Charli wanted no thanks from him.

"Oh, my receptionist. Great. Great, and very thoughtful." He smiled. It did nothing to alleviate her intense disliked for him, and giving him a glare she hoped would shrivel his gorgeous hair from the top of his equally gorgeous head, Charli marched out of his office.

She slumped into her chair and leaning her elbow on top of her desk, cupped her chin in her hand.

This was the worst thing that could happen. Tears flooded. She blinked them back. She didn't want to leave Knight Books. She loved her job and had thought she'd be here until retirement.

She'd been so prepared to work like a dog for the young Mr. Knight. Stand loyally by his side through thick and thin. He hadn't even given her a chance.

He'd said her name had confused him. So he'd thought her a man, and, obviously working alongside a woman, for the illustrious William Knight, was akin to working with a psychopath with hedonistic tendencies. And she knew why. Judy had told her about William Knight's ex and how she'd cut the matrimonial rug out from under him. So he was bitter? So he'd had a raw deal? Did that mean he had to punish every woman that came his way?

She had truly forgotten about the temporary part of her job. She'd been working so long in the capacity of CE it'd slipped her mind. Mr. Knight's original CE had found another job and practically walked out on him.

He'd always liked her, Charli knew this, and he'd placed her in the job of CE saying she was right for the job, and he knew they'd get on well together. He'd been so right.

How she wished she'd reminded Malcolm Knight that the job was only temporary. He'd have immediately made her position permanent. No use lamenting.

She ripped a tissue from the box and blew her nose. Feeling sorry for herself, she conjured up all the bad things that had happened to her in the last few years. Her mother's untimely death—at only forty-eight, her mother had succumbed to breast cancer. It had been difficult enough coming to terms with her death, but her father had dropped his bundle and withdrawn into the shadows, unable to cope with the grief.

Then, two years ago, there'd been that ghastly fling with Robert Bentley, a book distributor she'd met at a book fair. She had to be honest and say that she went into the affair with Robert because she wanted to lose her virginity. She wanted to know what sex was about and at twenty-one knew it was about time. He was handsome enough and she'd been attracted to him from the beginning, but her heart hadn't danced the tango at the mere sight of him and she definitely didn't hear bells when he'd kissed her.

He was okay in the courting department, but unromantic and, well, boring. He'd taken her out a few times. On the fourth date, she'd asked him over for dinner. Set the seduction scene. Candles, soft music, dimmed lights. Worn her sexiest dress. Fluttered her eyelashes at him throughout dinner until she was quite light-headed. Put her brain into storage and hung onto every word he spoke. Laughed at his not-so-funny jokes and when the final act came and she was in his arms, he'd made the confession.

He was gay. Not maybe gay but positively, over the fence gay. The reason he'd gone out with her was that he needed a woman to take to his sister's wedding. He hadn't told his parents about his sexual orientation. He needed a front.

Charli withdrew another tissue and dabbed her eyes. After that debacle with Robert, she'd taken the vow that she'd have to love the next man before sleeping with him. Trouble was the next man hadn't come along. She'd meet a man, he'd asked her for drinks at a pub, put the hard word on her, and when she refused she'd never hear from him again. Not that she'd wanted to.

She wanted so much more from a man, romantic dinners, dancing in the dark, holding hands in the back seat of the movies. She wanted him to get to know her and her him. His likes and dislikes, his favorite food, his taste in movies and music.

Was needing to be courted the crime of the century?

Anyway, she hadn't felt sparks. No ringing bells. No earth tremors.

Result. She was still a virgin. Most probably die a virgin.

She glanced over at William Knight's office door. Now when she'd finally met a man who made her heart dance, he turned out to be her worst enemy.

She wiped her eyes with the back of her hand. Enough tears already.

"Can we make lunch earlier? I don't think I can hold out till one."

Charli jumped. She hadn't realized Judy had come into the room.

Judy studied her face. "What's wrong?"

"The young Mr. Knight doesn't like me," she said.

"Whad-'d-ya mean?"

"Just what I'm saying." She blew her nose. "I'd forgotten this job was temp. He reminded me. He's going to advertise it." She sighed.

"No kidding? Oh yeah, I remember now you took over from June Haddock. Heck, what a damn mess. What happens now?"

"I go back to my old position."

"Eating crow don't taste so good."

Charli shrugged. "I've eaten it many times before. It'll be a five-minute wonder in the office until something juicier comes along."

"That's the spirit."

"He's going to advertise the job in-house and outside."

"Then go for it. You're sure to get it."

"I won't have a chance in hell. He wants a man working for him. You wait and see, Judy. He'll hire the first male CE that applies for the job."

"Because of what happened with his ex? She sure did a job on him."

"So that makes him a woman hater?"

"Not so much that he hates women, I've heard different on that score."

"Oh, so he's a love lord as well."

"Seems so. I can tell you stories that would melt the enamel from your teeth."

"So tell me."

"Not now, at lunch." Judy shook her head slightly. "I can understand him not trusting women in business."

"He could have given me a trial period at the very least."

"Not much you can do about it."

Charli wriggled in her chair. "I never imagined for one moment that Mr. Knight wouldn't want me. I thought we'd get on and things would stay the same. Instead I've got the bottom ripped out of my pants."

She raked a hand back through her hair and exhaled. "What sticks in my gut is that he wouldn't even give me the chance to prove myself to him. He's so inflexible."

"What are you going to do?"

"What every girl who's just been demoted does."

"Bite the bullet?"

"Find a witch and have a hex placed on the young Mr. Knight."
She closed her eyes, held up crossed fingers and intoned, "I wish
that William Knight gets one swift kick in his backside." She
opened one eye. "So hard he can't sit down for a week."

Chapter Four

Call each day to inquire about her health and well-being.

Charli woke early. Surprisingly, she'd slept well when she'd thought she'd toss and turn the whole night. Only once she'd woken, her mind full of William Knight. And she knew what she would do. She couldn't stay at Knight Books and watch another person do her job. It was too much for any woman to bear.

The autumn weather had turned unexpectedly warm. Through the open window, she could hear the twittering of birds. The soft morning light filtered through the open lace curtains. She stretched down the bed and wiggled her toes. How could she ever feel unhappy in this lovely room? She loved this room with its combination of wicker baskets and timber boxes and floor length curtains in an all-white color scheme creating a quiet, airy harbor away from all distractions. Double doors led onto a small balcony that boasted a lilac cane and wrought iron table and chairs where she spent most of her mornings drinking coffee and reading.

Throwing back the cover and shivering slightly as the cool air hit her naked body, she donned a woolen bathrobe and headed for the shower.

She had to work out which way to head. She had to decide whether she wanted to work in another publishing house or try something different. That was the troublesome question.

Grabbing the bottle of shampoo and squeezing a generous dollop into her cupped hand, she lathered her hair.

She didn't fancy starting a new job. Fitting in. Meeting new people. Learning the ropes. It didn't sit well with her. What could she do besides what she knew? Open a business? Like what? A teashop? Hmm, she couldn't even boil water successfully. Best she stay with what she knew best. A bookshop, now there was a great possibility. She personally knew many editors and writers and could ask—she wasn't past begging—them to do book signings and book readings.

Excitement stirred the pit of her tummy. She had her savings and she'd borrow whatever she could, and start Charli's Bookshop or Honey's Hardcovers. It'd be difficult because she was still paying off her flat and the mortgage payments were enough to choke a horse.

She rinsed the shampoo out of her hair and stepped out of the shower, grabbing a towel to dry off.

She padded into the bedroom and glanced out of the window. Because it was such a fine day, and because she was feeling so miserable, she decided to go for a jog around Albert Park Lake before work. It would shake away the cobwebs, maybe even convince her that what had happened was for the best and that her next adventure in life would be wonderfully exciting. And in a way it was exciting thinking about what she would do next. Which way to go? Whatever happened, she'd grab hold of it with both hands and do her best to be a success.

She placed a change of clothes into an oversized shoulder bag. She'd shower and change at work. She pinned her long hair into an untidy knot on the top of her head and not bothering with make-up, dressed in a pair of running shorts and skimpy T-shirt.

Charli glanced at the clock. Six thirty. She had plenty of time for her jog and time to give her father, who she knew arose at six every morning without fail, a quick hello. She desperately wanted to tell him she'd lost her job and how unhappy she was. Maybe she'd go to the farm for a few days to lick her wounds, give herself time to think over her next move.

She moved into the kitchen, poured herself a glass of icy-cold cranberry juice, and drained the glass in one long thirsty gulp.

She'd grab a coffee and croissant after her jog and eat it at work.

She worried about her father and his general health. Before her mother had died, he'd been a happy and carefree man full of laughter and love. He'd become a recluse, spurning her as well as his lifelong friends who, now tired of lame excuses, had stopped making allowances for him and ceased to call on him. She'd tried to reason with him. Tell him how much she needed him and wanted to be with him, but it was as if he'd lost contact with the real world, preferring instead to stay inside the dark and lonely world he'd created for himself.

She reached for the telephone and dialed her father's number. He answered on the second ring. "Hi, Dad. It's me."

"Hi, love, how are you?"

"Fine, how are you?"

"Good, good."

"I haven't seen you in such a long time, Dad. I was—"

"I've been busy here on the farm, love, and besides you're always at work and weekends you seem to have such a lot on. Still, it's what a young girl should be doing. Working and playing hard. The years go so fast you wonder where they've gone."

He sounded down. Miserable. She didn't know how to help him. What to do to get him back to life. "Dad, I was wondering if I could come up and visit for a few days?"

"When were you planning to come?"

"Soon. Maybe next week or the week after."

She sensed his hesitation, his reluctance to have her with him on the farm and her heart sank. "I don't know, love. I'm not sure what I'll be doing."

"You'd only be doing farm work and I can help you with that. I'd enjoy helping you, Dad."

"It's other things besides that, love. It's the town meeting, and I've got to go Echuca on farm business. I'm flat out."

"You wouldn't know I was there, I promise."

"Can you leave it for a few weeks? You know, until I'm feeling more like having people around."

People? She wound the telephone cord around her finger. "Sure, I understand."

"We'll make definite plans another time. Okay, love?"

"Yeah, Dad, another time."

"Love you."

"You, too. Bye, Dad. Bye." She placed the receiver onto the hook.

It was one rejection too many; and with a sob she sunk down to the floor, covered her face with her hands and sobbed.

Crying jag over, she sat with her back against the wall. Before her mother died, her father had been frantic for her to come to the farm. Not so now. Now he wanted to be alone with his wounds, pottering around the farm content in his misery, not intending ever to get over her mother's death it seemed. And Charli was helpless. What could she do? She'd tried to reason with him. Tell him that life must go on, what had happened had happened and nothing they could do or say would bring her mother back. She'd said these and all the other platitudes she could think of, but it was useless. Her father simply refused to stop mourning his wife.

Her nose was running and she didn't have the strength of character to get up and find a tissue. She wiped her nose with the inside hem of her T-shirt.

Okay, so she reminded him of her mother, and it pained him to look at her. But she needed to be with him, especially now when her life had cracked up in her face and she didn't know which way to go.

She struggled to her feet, walked down the corridor and into the bathroom where she washed her face of tears, ran her hand through her hair, and staring at her reflection in the mirror, murmured, "Bugger it."

She left the bathroom, walked back down the corridor and reached for her car keys and left her flat.

*

Reaching the park by seven, Charli parked her car and walked to the lake's edge. It was so peaceful, so calm, and absolutely perfect for a quiet jog. The blue water sparkled in the early morning sun. And the dark clouds floating around her head dispersed. She inhaled the sweet air deeply, feeling totally restored; the rest of her life wasn't going to be a mess; she knew, with quiet confidence, that she'd sort things out and everything would come out smelling of roses.

A few stray seagulls, seeking food left by the Sunday barbeques, wheeled in slow graceful circles, squawking loudly as she passed beneath them.

She'd been jogging for a few minutes when, in the distance, another jogger appeared. By the massive width of the shoulders, it was definitely a man.

She slowed her pace but kept her movement smooth. She tripped over her own feet. The other jogger was her sworn adversary. William Knight apparently had the same idea as her about an early morning jog. She quickened her pace.

Oh my God, this is so embarrassing. What should I do? Ignore him like he didn't exist? Give him a wave and jog on past? Smile and yell out, good morning, great day for a jog isn't it?

She didn't wish him well. She wished him to the devil. She'd jog past him with nose held firmly in the air; as if her demotion hadn't shattered her confidence; as if she lost her job every day of her life and it meant nothing to her.

If William Knight were the last human on earth with her, she'd prefer the company of a man-eating ravenous crocodile. Preferred scenario, William Knight's left leg in said crocodile's mouth.

He halted and glared down at her as if she was somehow taking up his space. She had no alternative but to stop.

He looked her up and down with breathtaking audacity, a cheeky grin on his handsome face.

He was standing far too close for comfort, and Charli found something about him disabling. She wasn't sure if it was the tuft of coal black hair falling down his forehead or the emerald glint in his magnificent eyes or maybe the sensual curve to his mouth. Whatever he had it was more than enough. Her heart was beating way too fast.

She attempted to move past without being too obvious. She didn't want him aware of the effect he had on her. He was arrogant enough without adding her fascination to his I'm-too-good-for-this-world list of self-wonders.

She wondered if he had a girlfriend or if he dated at whim. Then she reasoned that he didn't have a thing to worry about, he'd simply choose from the line of panting women waiting outside his front door.

Well, not this little black duck, no sirree Bob. She panted after no man. She was pant-less. Her head jerked back. Thank God, she hadn't spoken that little gem aloud. What a joke William Knight would have had on that unintentional pun.

Slightly out of breath still, she placed her hands on her hips and glared defiantly at him. And he smiled. The creep had the audacity to grin as if he knew something that she did not. Arrogant, smug, half-witted baboon. She fought the impulse to smack him fair in the chin.

He lowered his eyes and attached them to her T-shirt. Printed in large black letters was BAD GIRL, T-SHIRT.

"Like your shirt."

Charli sniffed. Who gives a rat's whisker what you like. "A Christmas gift from Judy, she has a weird sense of humor," she explained.

"Judy?"

"She's your receptionist."

"Oh, yes, the flower lady. Has she been working for us long?"

"Ten years or so."

31

"Didn't know you were into jogging."

"Why, is it a male orientated past-time?"

He grinned. "No, of course not, but you didn't seem the type to go in for jogging."

"What type am I, Mr. Knight?" This man irritated her like a bee buzzing around your head or a mosquito biting your ankle. You swatted both.

"I thought you'd be more into arty things."

"Yeah? Like what?"

"Painting. Ballet. Opera. You know."

"And you say that on a one-meeting basis? You amaze me. I had no idea that you're an expert on human nature. You must tell me more." She nodded, considering. "Do you tell fortunes, Mr. Knight?"

How dare he chat away with her like she was his long lost cousin? Did he expect her to be civil when he'd so cruelly tossed her aside?

She wished with all her might that she could get a terrific job with his competition and make their sales go through the roof. Securing wonderfully clever writers the world over screaming to be read. She'd meet him at book functions and she'd smile sweetly at him, and say, hear you're going downhill fast. Too bad, Mr. Knight, them's the breaks.

He moved in closer and heat, which now had nothing to do with jogging, rose in her body. Her voice quaked. "Would you kindly remove your bulk so I can continue on around the park?" With a slight flip to her head, she sidestepped him.

His big hand snaked across and took her hand. The moment his hand touched hers a jolt of fire shot through her. Her heart hammered. Electricity sparked between them. Her eyes flew wide open. The blood rushed up her neck and burst into her face.

He stared at her in astonishment, his mouth agape as if he'd seen the eighth wonder of the world. Had he received the same electrifying shock when his fingers had touched hers? Then, when she was thinking that maybe he was human after all, his eyes shaded and the same let-nobody-know-what-I'm-thinking bloke stood in front of her.

With supreme effort, Charli convinced herself it was her natural dislike for this man causing such discomfort. She glared. "Kindly release my hand," she said. "I don't like being mauled."

She didn't have to be polite or even nice. She'd made up her mind what she was about to do. Run—leaving the big-headed William Knight to stew in his own juice. Charli had reasoned that he needed her, at least for a while. Show him where they were at. Tell him about their established authors and the ones still in the pipeline. New releases, oh so much that her head swirled thinking of it.

Let him learn the hard way. She ignored the feeling of meanness that almost overcame her, consoling herself that he'd thrown her to the wolves without pity.

He released her hand, his eyes flicked again across the writing on her T-shirt. He lowered his head and she had the amazing sensation he was going to kiss her. She tensed, her hand curling into a small fist.

"Who are you?" he whispered.

"What?"

"Where did you come from?"

She didn't understand his questions. Didn't know what was going on between them except for this raw primitive hunger that seemed to stem from him and enter her. She was scared. She couldn't handle the situation. She wanted to put as much distance as humanly possible between her and William Knight.

"Mr. Knight," she said, as if trying to explain the beginning of time to a six-year-old. "I came out this morning to enjoy a quiet jog around the lake. I am not in the mood for early morning bantering with you or anyone. If you wish to continue this conversation, I suggest we do so on your time. This is my private time and I'd appreciate keeping it just that."

"Ah, but you see, Honey, your time is my time."

"Yeah? Explain that to me."

"The wages I pay you."

"I'm paid for the time I work," she said. She hated this man with an intensity that set her teeth aching. She idly wondered how many years you got for justifiable homicide and what the hell she could use for a weapon.

"No, not quite," he said and either the sun was glinting in his eyes or they were twinkling. They were amazing eyes; crystal clear and sparkling like jewels. "If you read the CE job specification you'd see that your extraordinarily large wage entitles me to your services when and where I deem necessary."

"I think a lawyer might put a slightly different interpretation on that clause and as I neither have a manuscript or as much as a pencil tucked inside my shorts, Mr. Knight, I find it rather difficult to believe you need my services at this precise moment."

His gaze lowered. "Hmm, you're so right, there's absolutely no room."

No matter what she said, he drew her back into reminding her she was a woman. "As much as I am enjoying this stimulating conversation, I'm beginning to freeze, so if you don't mind—"

He gave a bow to his dark head. "I've no shackles around you, Honey,"

She had to have the last word even though deep down she knew it was useless, that somehow William Knight would always come up trumps. "It appears to me that you seem intent on looking for trouble?"

"I never got anything worthwhile without trouble."

"Only because of the way you choose to live," she said. "I myself like a more sedate type of life."

"Sedate or boring?"

"My life is neither boring nor any of your business," she said.

She couldn't despise this man more if he were talking her into buying an unwanted set of outdated encyclopedias. He'd coolly taken her job from her and now he was speaking to her like they were as familiar as old friends. Familiar? She'd like to get as close to him as she would a cane toad with measles.

He made to touch her again and she spat the words at him. "Don't touch me. I warn you I practice Krav Maga."

He laughed and anger flamed her brain. She made to move away, stumbled and fell into his arms, her body hard against his. He held her tight. His eyes connected with hers. And she recalled the time when the fire alarm had gone off at work and panic had ensued. The same chest-tightening fear, the same sense of unreality that she was in a situation she couldn't handle.

His head lowered and his lips brushed hers. All the breath left her body at the mere anticipation of his kiss. He claimed her mouth. The kiss was electric. Her whole body responded. She wrapped her arms around his neck as she thrust herself closer to the power of him. His kiss was sweet and beyond forgetting.

Bells rang.

Her toes sizzled inside her sneakers.

Totally hot.

"Honey." He whispered her name. She ignored the heat burning in her groin and that she wanted, with all her might, to kiss him again and again, because to tell the truth she was scared witless. She'd been kissed before—no, retract that, she'd never been kissed until William Knight had kissed her.

A fireball sizzled around her heart. She was totally alive and vital. The colors surrounding her took on a more vivid hue. She sighed and raised her face to his, waiting for his next kiss.

A small triumphant laugh and her senses returned in a bolt of savage lightning.

She jerked away from him. Humiliation replaced desire. She wiped her hand across her burning lips. "You—you, presumptuous twerp."

He had the decency to look stunned and she wondered if the kiss had rocked him as much as it had her. Yeah, and cows can dance rock and roll. This man was a student of Casanova.

"I'm sorry, I don't know why I did that. Please, forget that ever happened," he said.

Forget? How could she forget the taste of his mouth on hers? How could she forget the sensation of being held in his arms? Forget the wash of sexual desire that had flooded her like a tidal wave?

She took a vow that today was positively the last day she'd come into contact with him. After today she'd never have to think of William Knight. He'd be a nasty little memory tucked away in the black regions of her memory and deep concentration and a lot of yoga could eventually erase him from there.

"Forget what?" She moved past him and broke into a quick run.

She glanced over her shoulder. He was out of sight. She stopped. Holding her sides, she took deep breaths until her breathing returned to normal. She walked back to her car, opened the car door, and reached inside for her towel. She quickly wiped the perspiration from her body, threw the towel onto the car seat, slipped in behind the wheel and headed for Knight Books.

Only one day. She could do that standing on her head.

Couldn't she?

Chapter Five

Buy her a new bonnet from Paris; a Cavalier King Charles Spaniel, housetrained of course.

Charli typed out her resignation. Signed it. Placed it in an envelope and put it into William Knight's urgent matters file. *Done deal. No more regrets. Forward ever forward into the mighty unknown.*

She didn't know how long it'd take to get another position. Maybe it would be good if she took a holiday. Nowhere expensive. Maybe take a bus tour through South Australia, or New South Wales, or maybe catch the ferry to Tasmania, hire a car, and explore the island. She knew what she really wanted to do, so badly. She wanted to be with her dad, talk to him about her feelings, wander around the farm, and catch up with old school friends. Get her mind right.

Dad doesn't want me. Another unwelcomed gush of self-pity enfolded her. For God's sake, shape up.

Judy entered her office. She glanced at the envelope. "Is that what I think it is?"

"Yes."

"So you've decided to leave."

"I can't work with him, Judy. He's impossible."

"Fair enough."

"I feel so darn low."

"Hey, so you lost your job. It's not the end of the world. You've still got me."

She smiled. "Yes, thank God. We'll always be mates." She took a deep breath. "I'm thinking about taking a holiday. Nowhere special. Just get away and get my head right."

"Sounds the way to go. A holiday always makes me feel good."

"I hate him." The words were out of her mouth before she could control them. Whatever would Judy think of her now?

"That's a trifle strong."

She'd gone too far to stop now. "He's mean and authoritarian and arrogant and bull-headed and selfish, and, and—"

"And the boss," Judy finished for her. "Cheer up, Charli. Maybe it's for the best. Maybe you'll find the job of the century and laugh about this as the joke of the century."

"Oh, Judy, don't throw me platitudes. Not from you, it's too damn much."

She laughed. "Sorry. How about lunch? My shout. I'll take you to Flower Drum, your favorite Cantonese restaurant. You can stuff yourself with crab meat vermicelli clay pot and seafood rice paper rolls."

Charli's mouth watered at the thought. "You sure know how to tempt a girl."

"I know the way to your heart is through your stomach. I've never known a girl to eat as much as you and still stay slim."

"It's in my genes. And there's no way I can resist the wonderful food of Flower Drum. Count me in."

"I'll book just to be sure. See you at one."

Charli pressed the intercom. "May I see you, Mr. Knight?"

"Yeah, sure. Come in, Honey."

She flicked off the intercom and poked out her tongue. "Come in, Honey," she mimicked. "Rude ape." She took a silent vow not to let him upset her in any way, shape, or form. She'd be cool and sophisticated. Show him what a pearl he was losing.

Picking up her letter of resignation, she knocked once on his door and entered his inner sanctum. He looked up and indicated the chair in front of his desk with his pen. Her top lip curled into a sneer. She despised this man with an intensity that made her want to kick his shin.

Sitting demurely on a chair opposite his, she straightened her skirt, tugging it over her knees as best she could seeing it was a mini skirt and refused to budge more than an inch. She thought about crossing her legs and giving him a glimpse of her long and slim nylon clad legs. She'd love him to stare at them with his tongue hanging out.

She stared at the top of his head as he finished off his paperwork.

"Sorry about this. Won't be a moment," he mumbled.

She looked at his hands, strong and surprisingly tanned. She liked them. Her eyes flew to his face, with his eyes downcast toward the paper she could see the clean sweep of his eyelashes and gasped inwardly at their thickness and length.

He's practically perfect. She searched for a flaw. There had to be something, a birthmark, an ugly mole, anything, she'd settle for a pimple but he was perfection.

Without raising his eyes, he spoke. "You wanted to see me?"

She handed him her resignation. "I think you'll find this self-explanatory."

He glanced up at her, the force of his personality italicized by the gentle husky tone and took the proffered letter. "So you've decided to leave us?"

Charli suppressed her flash of anger. "I didn't have that much choice."

"I was hoping you'd stay. If not in your old position, in some other capacity. It's nothing personal, Honey."

Liar, liar. It was so personal it was a crime. If she wanted she could take him to the discrimination board and fight it out and most probably win. Then what? She'd be working under such dreadful conditions. Him resenting her, she nervous and inept because she couldn't concentrate on her work, and she'd finally end up either leaving or asking to be transferred to another position. So nothing gained, nothing lost.

"Nothing personal?" she said. "You throw me to the wolves and say it's not personal. Really, Mr. Knight, I think you live in a fool's paradise. You neither gave me a chance to show you what I can do, or allowed me time to convince you of my capabilities."

He was about to say something to her when his phone rang. "Excuse me," he said as he lifted the receiver. "Knight," he barked and she wondered if he lacked the capacity to talk civilly to anyone. "Yes…yes…yes…I understand…eight-thirty. Fine." He disconnected and stared at her in such a way she thought one of her eyebrows had dropped off.

"My uncle's will is being read tonight."

His uncle's will? What was that to her? Why didn't he simply shake her hand and say her wages would be posted. "Oh, that's nice," she said.

"The solicitors request your presence, Honey."

She pointed to her chest with one finger. "Me?"

"It appears you are a beneficiary."

"I'm a beneficiary?"

"Honey, you have the irritating habit of repeating everything I say."

"Sorry. I was surprised that's all. I didn't imagine that Mr. Knight would leave me anything."

He grinned and her stomach did a war dance. "My mother is also a beneficiary but I know she'll refuse to go. Wills are too final, she tells me." He chuckled and Charli's lips responded in a sickly smile. "I'll stand in as her representative." He stood and she followed suit. "I'll pick you up around eight."

"I can make my own way, thanks."

"Don't be ridiculous."

She mentally shrugged. "About my resignation. I can't see the point in staying out the week. I'd like to leave at the end of this working day."

She didn't want to be here a moment longer than necessary. She couldn't take the pitying stares of the staff, the rush around to get her a gift. She wanted to leave without any fuss, as if she'd never worked at Knight Books.

"If that's your choice, that suits me fine."

Yeah, I bet it does. Miserable, she walked from his office and slumped into her chair.

That's that then, a closure of her time at Knight Books. Oh, well, there's good in every bad. At least she'd never see the smirking face of William Knight again. Oh my God, he was picking her up at eight and she'd have to spend a few more hours with him; misery descended like a pack of wolves.

Chapter Six

Never stop courting her.

William Knight stood there, his massive frame diminishing her doorway. *This is the last time I'll have to see him. After tonight, he'll just be a nasty memory.*

"I'm early. I took the chance that you may be ready."

"Ready?"

"The solicitors."

"Solicitors?"

"Honey, maybe you should see someone about that habit of yours."

Reason restored, she drew back, embarrassed, flustered, her heart beating painfully in her breast. "I'm sorry. I'm not quite ready. Would you mind coming in?"

"Not at all." He pushed past her and entering the living room, threw himself into a large sofa chair.

She followed him into the room. "Can I offer you coffee, Mr. Knight? Something stronger?"

"Coffee would be great. And for the record, my friends call me Will. If it's challenging for you to be that personal, call me William. Calling me mister makes me feel ancient."

She didn't answer him, but he was correct in his assumption that it would be difficult for her to call him by his first name; it was far too intimate. It automatically stopped their association from being what she wanted to keep it, totally detached. And as far as calling him Will, well, there were quite a few names she'd have liked to call him.

She tilted her head. She could be adult about the situation. She'd show him how she handled the bad parts of her life. With decorum and a deep spirit of womanhood. She had accepted the challenge Fate had bestowed on her and was willing to face whatever lay ahead. Her shoulders sagged. Who was she kidding? Brave words did not a future make. Sometimes it took months to find decent employment. A flutter of panic arose somewhere at the base of her throat. She swallowed. She had her severance pay. That would last a few months if she were extremely careful.

She glanced over at the man sitting casually in her best chair. He looked like he didn't have a care in the world. Hell, he didn't. Still she supposed she couldn't blame him for that. "I'll make the coffee...Will."

He grinned. "See, Honey, that wasn't so hard, was it?"

Smart aleck. Her chin went up, anger rising. She tossed her hair. "My mother always told me to be polite, even to people I don't like."

He had the cheek to laugh long and hard. Her blood bubbled in her veins. Wasn't there any way she could outdo this man? She craved to get the better of him, to have that final sweet soul-salving triumph of seeing him brought to his knees.

The room dissolved...

Sitting behind a desk at Knight Books, Will approaches me, hat in hand, no, falling to his knees in front of me, begging for his job. "You can take a severance package or stay as toilet janitor, the choice is yours, buddy."

He takes my hand inside his and drags me down to the floor beside him. With a sigh, he clasps me to him, his lips pressed on mine with a demanding kiss of such passion and delight that every hair on my body stands on end and—

"Maybe I should make the coffee, Honey?"

The dream dissolved. "What?"

"You were staring at me like I had two heads."

Yeah, and both of them magnificent. "Sorry. I'll make it now."

*

An hour later, she was walking into the solicitor's office with Will. At the lateness of the hour, Alex Jordan was alone. He greeted them and ushered them into his office.

"Thank you both for coming," the solicitor said needlessly. As if for some odd reason neither would be interested in what Malcolm Knight's will said. She, for one, was bursting to find out what Mr. Knight had left her. It had to be money. Her stomach sank. Oh God, it wasn't that awful painting his wife had done at art class still hanging on his office wall. The one Charli had always pretended to admire because she knew it had pleased him for her to do so.

Will settled into a chair on one side of the room, and Charli chose a chair on the other side, as far away from Will as humanly possible. "Besides my mother, are we the only beneficiaries?" Will asked.

"Yes." Alex Jordan sat behind a huge desk, donned horn-rimmed glasses, picked up a legal looking document, and cleared his throat. "Shall we begin?"

They both nodded.

"This is the last Will and Testament of Maxwell George Knight of 278 Bellbird Crescent, Kew, in the State of Victoria.

"I hereby revoke all Wills heretofore made by me.

"I appoint Alex Jordan, of Jordan, Smith & Willis, Solicitors at Law, as my executor and Trustee of this, my Will.

"I make the following specific Bequests: That my sister-in-law, Ester Knight, be left my house in Kew along with all my personal belongings.

"That my business Knight Books and all my monies be left to my nephew, William Malcolm Knight."

"That my Chief Editor, Charli Elizabeth Honey be left $20,000."

Charli let out an audible gasp. "Mr. Knight has left me $20,000?"

"It appears so, Miss Honey," Alex Jordan replied.

"Wow, that's a tidy sum," Will said, glancing at Charli. "What did you do to get him to leave you $20,000?"

Charli drew herself erect in her chair. "What are you suggesting?"

He shrugged. "Why would he leave you such an amount? Unless—"

Her face grew hot. The insufferable moralistic germ. "Unless I slept with him. Is that what you're suggesting, *Mr. Knight*?"

He had the grace to look ashamed. "No, of course not. I just wondered that's all," he finished lamely.

"The relationship between your uncle and me was strictly business." She glared at him. "The same as is between us, and will always remain between us for as long as God grants me life."

"Hey, you don't have to be so dramatic."

"I'm not being dram—"

"Miss Honey, Mr. Knight, if you please. It's late and I'd like to get home."

They both apologized.

*

They barely spoke on the way back to her flat. "Can I come in for coffee?"

"I see no need for further conversation, Mr. Knight. We've said all that's necessary."

He ignored her. "There's something I need to say to you and sitting in the car isn't the right place to do it."

She shrugged her consent.

He silently followed her up the path, inside the building, up a flight of stairs, and inside her apartment. She walked into the kitchen. He followed suit sitting on a hard-back chair at the kitchen table. She took the cups and saucers from the cupboard and made coffee. Shuffling some chocolate-coated biscuits onto a plate, she placed the steaming mug and plate of biscuits in front of him. She took a seat opposite him.

Will shifted on the edge of his chair and Charli's eyes went to his powerful, firm, well-shaped thighs. Dragging her eyes away from them to focus on his beautiful eyes, Charli said, "What is it you want to say to me?"

"I want to apologize for my bad behavior in the solicitor's office, Honey."

"Stop calling me Honey."

"That's your name."

"My name is Charli or Miss Honey." She squirmed in her chair. He noticed her discomfort and grinned.

"Why are you so upset?"

"I'm not upset."

"It's only a name."

"It's the way you say it."

"How do I say it?" That infuriating smirk.

One day, so help me God, I'm going to wipe that smirk right off his face.

"Syrupy."

"As in honey, Honey?" He laughed at his own weak joke. Really, this man was the limit. One moment he was as serious as a judge passing a life sentence and the next doing a poor imitation of Groucho Marx.

"I like women's names to sound like they belong to women. I like my women feminine."

"And you think I care?" she said. "This is so typical of you to assume that what you like everybody else automatically should like."

"I was merely commenting on your name," he said and the quietness of his tone infuriated her even more.

"I would prefer you to keep your comments to yourself. I find them neither interesting nor informative."

He frowned. "Your parents must have had an inkling about your personality to have given you a boy's name."

She drew herself erect her eyes blazing fire at him. "I was named after my grandfather who happened to have died on the day I was born."

"It's a pity your grandfather hadn't been called Elizabeth or something as equally feminine," he said.

"You always have double sets of standards," she said smugly, pleased with her analogy. "One for you and the other for anyone else that who may be in your life at the time."

He spoke as if her foregoing sentence had never been uttered and she was slightly crestfallen. Why could she never get the best of this man? No matter what she said he had a rejoinder.

"Is that a fact?" He gulped down the remainder of his coffee. "Any more coffee?"

"Sure." She stood and filled his cup. She resumed her seat and her mind wandered. She would bring him to his knees, somehow, some way.

She'd power dress the way the women did in the movies. Wear heavy-rimmed glasses and allow no man, especially William Knight to overawe her. A scene flashed into her mind…

Dressed in a long jacket, mini-skirt suit wearing spike heel shoes, mobile phone in one hand and a black coffee in the other, I stride into Knight Books yelling out orders.

Will opens his office door and the look of admiration bubbles my coffee. "You look absolutely gorgeous," he said as he winds his arm around my waist and drags me into his office. "You drive me crazy. I have to have you or go mad."

I'm held in those strong arms. His body presses against mine; listening to his passionate words of love; his big hands all over my body. My hands move across his taut muscles, our need for each other overpowering our need to breathe. Nothing exists except our touches, our desires. Our lovemaking...

Charli's nipples tightened.

"Bloody hell. Honey, are you with me?"

She blinked. "Excuse me?"

"You've got this strange habit of staring off into space. It's weird."

"I was thinking."

"Yeah? Well, I've seen concentration before but you take the cake. It's like you're off in some dream world."

"The way I stare, act, or respond is none of your business."

"Is there anything you should tell me?"

She bristled. "What are you talking about?"

He grinned. "Eccentricities in the family? Skeletons in the closet? Anything you want to share with me?"

"My family is from good Australian stock and proud of it."

Without warning, he took her hand inside his, dragging her closer to him. She wanted to pull away. Honest she did. But he held her mesmerized with the wicked wonderful gleam in his eyes.

"Just now when you were talking about your family," he said with a smile that lifted her heart and turned it upside-down. "You looked like an avenging angel."

"Angel?"

He laughed softly. "Perhaps I should have said witch. Witches cast spells, don't they?"

"Evil spells," she said.

"Are you casting an evil spell around me, Honey?"

Charli became edgy with the proceeding conversation. They weren't saying anything that really meant anything, yet somehow their words were electrified with intimacy. She shot her answer at him. "I think you have me confused with someone else."

His lips brushed her hair. She trembled. "I don't think that would be possible," he said.

He raised a hand and lifted a wisp of her hair from her cheek and tucked it behind her ear. Her body quivered. She tugged her hand from his and moved backwards. What disturbed her the most was the racing of her heart, the shortness of her breath and the tingling sensation on her ear where his fingers had lightly brushed the skin.

Suddenly his lips were close to hers. She couldn't take another one of his kisses. She would melt.

What were her true feelings for this man? She was so confused. One minute she hated him with an intensity that bewildered her, and the next she wanted him to kiss her with that same mystifying intensity. Was this love?

Before she could stop him—did she really want to?—his arm wound tightly around her waist, pulling her into him. Her body fused to his. "Hear my heart?" he said softly. "Hear it beating? It's pounding for you."

Whatever else she planned to say was lost as his mouth clamped down on hers, parting her lips with demanding force. Then suddenly his mouth was soft, yet insistent.

Oh. My. God.

She twisted her mouth away, but his lips followed hers and she pulsated under the power of his kiss. This time she had no intention of letting him go. She sighed against his mouth, wrapped her arms tightly around his neck and kissed him hard and long.

He held her gently, tracing his fingertips slowly up and down the curve of her spine as their kiss deepened. Heat spread though her bloodstream as his mouth moved over hers to imprison the very soul of her.

Her eyes fluttered closed, and her pulse throbbed plainly in the small groove at the base of her throat.

She forgot everything.

There was nothing left in the world but Will and what he was doing to her.

He kissed the tip of her nose, then her forehead, and her cheeks. She took his face between her hands and said, "Kiss me here." And she dragged his head down until his mouth connected with hers in a kiss that had the power to destroy the world.

Sensations fell upon her and she succumbed to them willingly. They lost control.

Will's hands slid along her ribs, over the outer curve of her breasts and down her hips.

Charli's hands were massaging the strength of his shoulders; relishing the feel of hard muscle and tendons beneath. Her heart, her stomach, her groin all played a magical game of their own.

He unbuttoned her blouse.

She slipped his coat from his shoulders. It fell to the floor and joined with her blouse.

She felt his coolness against the warmth of her skin, his seeking hands finding her breasts. He fumbled with the hooks of her bra while she unbuttoned his shirt.

And he kissed her again. Unrestrained, mercilessly, as if he wanted to control her with his kisses. He kissed her forehead, her eyes, her throat and back to her eager mouth. She couldn't get enough of him. She touched her tongue upon his lips. And then, in a wild flash of passion, she took hold of his head and drew him to her breast. He licked the darkening nipple, suckled it.

Both naked from the waist up they clamped together. His fingers touched her skin. The sensation was beyond imagination. An exquisite tenseness coiled around her. She wanted Will and she wanted him now.

He swept her into his arms. "Where's the bedroom?"

She jerked a thumb over one shoulder. "Down the hall. The last room on the right."

He carried her down the hall, kicked open the door, and placed her down on the bed. He lay next to her, curling her into his arms. His skin against hers. Delicious.

And then he was kissing every part of her. The breath caught in her throat as emotion upon emotion flooded her. She was being transported to heaven. "Touch me," Charli whispered.

His hand caressed her breast. "Here?" His fingers drifted along her ribs and belly to rest lightly on the climax of her thighs. "Or here?"

Charli let out an excited gasp. "Oh, yes," she murmured. "Yes, yes, yes."

His kiss was passionate and long and they moved in a sensuous rhythm. There was no beginning, no end to them. They were one. Each delighting in pleasing the other.

He entered her, and when he moved inside her their hands clasped together and she was transported to another world, a world that belonged to her and Will.

Her climax came with soul-tearing excitement and she knew, she was at last, a woman in every sense of the word.

He rolled from her and gave a small laugh. "Never thought I'd end up in your bed. This is the last place I expected to be."

And his words hurt her. Made her realize what they had done. It hadn't been special for Will. Not like for her. She clenched her hands so tightly her fingernails bit into the soft skin of her palm.

He'd wanted sex and she'd been handy. Swine. He was a user from way back. Creep.

Sanity crept into her brain. What was she doing, for heaven's sake? One minute she was screaming that she'd never sleep with him, and here she was curled up in his arms like some contented cat.

Shame descended. How could she have made love with such a callous man; a man who couldn't care less who was in his bed as long as it was a woman.

So, in her shame she spoke harshly, foolishly. "Please leave my bedroom," she said in a tone not unlike a ravished maiden in an historical novel.

"What?"

"I said, get out, you sex maniac." Brown eyes stared into green. "Don't think I'm always going to be that easy, mate."

"What the hell's going on?"

"You attacked me when my defenses were down."

"Attacked you? You almost bruised me out there in the kitchen."

"I don't wish to discuss it."

"I bet you don't."

"Kindly get dressed and leave my flat."

"With pleasure, lady," he said, scrambling from the bed, dressing quickly.

A feeling of dismay engulfed her as he stamped down the passage. She cringed at the slamming of the front door. She'd allowed things to go too far. Why hadn't she controlled the situation?

Because she'd wanted Will to make love to her.

Chapter Seven

The man pursues the woman.

It was over three weeks since she last saw Will. He'd tried telephoning her a few times but she'd refused to speak with him, hanging up as soon as she heard his voice. Once he'd come around to the flat. She'd hid in the kitchen until he gave up and went away. She knew he wanted to see her, at worst, apologize. She couldn't take that. Hold out her hand and say, forget it ever happened, I have. Oh, so not true.

There'd be nothing gained in seeing Will again. He was so not the man for her. No romance in his veins, a real bed-hopper. A man who'd forget your name by the time he'd left your house.

And as for job hunting she'd come up zilch, and she had to admit she was beginning to worry. Oh, she had the money left to her by Malcolm Knight and her savings, but paying her rent each month ate into it, and there were always the dreaded bills that were like a tidal wave that nothing could stop. She'd tried to work out how long her money would last, but it seemed that as soon as she budgeted, somehow it didn't work out and she had less in her bank account than she'd bargained for.

She sat at the kitchen table, feeling despondent, low enough to cut a snail's toenails. She was doodling on a pad, thinking of nothing in particular, when an electric shock shook her brain. She hadn't had her period. Her eyes flew to the calendar. She always circled the date and she was always, always on time. She jumped from her chair and raced to the calendar.

She fell back against the kitchen wall, dropped to the floor in a crouch, her trembling knees lacking the strength to hold her. She was almost a month overdue.

Oh, shit, oh, God, oh, bloody hell, no way. She couldn't be pregnant. It couldn't be true.

Okay, okay, breathe deeply. Don't panic, you're lost if you panic. Relax. Think more clearly.

Maybe the stress of the past few weeks had spun her body out of whack. She'd read somewhere that a woman hadn't menstruated for over a year after her parents had been killed in a car crash.

Charli needed proof. Grabbing her purse and car keys, she left the house for the nearest pharmacy.

*

Charli couldn't take her eyes from the pregnancy test. It only took a couple of minutes, yet to her it seemed hours. "Please, please, please show minus." Then, under her distressed and anxious eyes, came the dreaded plus sign.

Charli slumped onto the toilet, head cradled in her hands. It couldn't be. Oh dear God, she was pregnant. Her first instinct was to race around the bathroom like a chicken with its head cut off. Don't panic, whatever you do, don't panic.

She moved from the bathroom to the kitchen and put on the kettle. She had no job, no prospects. How could she raise a child?

Tears stung, she blinked them back. She'd go to the farm with her dad. Except her dad wouldn't understand why she was pregnant in the first place and where was the father, and why wasn't he marrying her? If she raved on about love, her dad would toss that aside with a growl, and tell her the most important thing was the protection and care of the baby.

It would destroy her dad more, and he was so darn low trying to get over her mum's passing.

She had two choices. Abort or keep the baby.

She had one choice and she knew it. No way could she abort her child, it wasn't a thing she could do.

The telephone rang. "Hello?"

"Hi, it's me. Wanna meet for lunch?"

"Judy. Can you come here and I'll make us some toasted cheese?"

"Aww, I was thinking grilled fish and salad."

"Then you bring lunch here."

"Something wrong?"

"Just get here quick."

*

They'd finished lunch and having their coffee when Judy said, "What's up, kiddo? You look down in the dumps."

"I'm pregnant," Charli blurted and burst into a flood of tears.

Her friend raced around and threw her arms around Charli's shoulders. "Oh hell, you poor duck." She moved a little away, patting Charli's hand. "Who's the bastard responsible?"

Charli took a tissue from her pocket and blew her nose. "He was just a one-night stand."

"Even so, you must have at least known his name."

"I—it's not important."

"Not important? What are you, the sacrificial victim of the year? Now 'fess up, who's the daddy?"

"Will."

"Will who?"

"The boss, Will, that's who."

Judy's mouth gaped open. "William Knight? He's the father? Bloody hell. How did it happen?"

"What do you mean, how did it happen? The way it always happens. We had sex."

"Yeah, I know that, I meant how did it happen between you and Will? You don't even like the bloke."

"It just happened. We didn't plan it."

Judy scratched her head. "I'm totally confused. I mean did you go to a hotel? What? Where? How?"

"Old Mr. Knight left me some money, and Will came over to talk about it. One minute we were talking about this and that and the next he was in my bed."

"Oh, shit. So what are you going to do about it?"

"Nothing."

"Don't be daft. The man's loaded. He had his fun now, he's gotta pay the price."

"He doesn't give a rat's arse about me or the baby. I haven't spoken to him since that night." That wasn't altogether a lie—after all, she'd refused to speak to him. Her conscience got the better of her. "Well, he did try a couple of times to speak to me."

"Why wouldn't you speak to him?"

"I didn't want to, that's why. There's nothing between us that's stable, or even the tiniest bit romantic."

"So what? Bugger that. He's got to face his responsibilities. It's not as if you raped him, is it?"

Charli laughed through her tears. "Hardly. He's built like a brick outhouse."

"Tell him, Charli, he has the right to know."

"I will tell him."

"When?"

"Soon."

Judy sighed. "What a bloody mess. What can I do to help?"

Charli shook her head. "This is my problem and I'll work it out."

Chapter Eight

Do not cause offense toward her family.

Charli climbed out of the bath, wrapped herself in a large towel, and headed for her bedroom. An early night and a good book was the order of the day. She dried herself off, slipped on her Bugs Bunny pjs and slid her feet into slippers shaped like a carrot. Another gift from Judy.

She headed for the kitchen to make herself a hot chocolate when the doorbell rang. "Damn, who could it be at this hour?" She shuffled her way to the door, and through her peephole stared at the creature from hell on her doorstep. He looked bedraggled as if he hadn't slept for a week. She refused to feel sympathy for him. "What do you want?" she called through the letter slot.

"We need to talk. I intend to wait here until you let me in."

Charli chewed her bottom lip.

"Let me in, Honey." He banged the door with his fist. "I mean it. I won't budge from your doorstep."

"Okay, okay, don't break down the door," she said as she opened it and allowed him entrance.

There was dark fire in his eyes and a fine chill threaded through her. He was as mad as a maniac with a meat axe.

"When were you going to tell me? Next week, next month, next bloody year? I've got a share in this baby too. He's my child."

She held up her hands. "Now don't go off half-cocked." She turned and shuffled back into the kitchen. "I'm making hot chocolate, want one?"

He almost fell into a chair, elbow on the table, holding his forehead with one hand. "I had to hear about the baby from my receptionist."

Damn Judy. She should have known she'd blab. Maybe on another level she had known that Judy would tell Will and maybe this was what she'd wanted her to do. "I didn't think you'd be interested in me or the baby."

He raised his stricken face. "Don't be so bloody stupid. "

She sat opposite him, contrite. "I'm sorry, Will, I should have been the one to tell you."

He grinned. Her heart melted. "The main thing is I know now. The next thing is what to do about the situation?"

She shrugged.

"You're financially strapped?" he said.

She straightened in her chair. "I have enough money to last a year."

"I've thought this over carefully, Honey. I want to be involved in my child's birth and his life. Therefore, I'm involved with yours."

She began to splutter. He held up one hand. "You have two choices. Listen well to me, Honey, because it is what it is and nothing you can say or do will alter it. Are you with me so far?"

She nodded.

"Good, good. First choice. I support you financially until after the baby is born and until you find suitable employment. I can help you there also. I will, of course, always support my child both emotionally and financially. That's a given."

"And the second choice is?"

"Marry me."

She choked, coughed, blinked her eyes and said, "That idea is intolerable. This is going from bad to worse. The answer is an unequivocal no."

"Hear me out. Being a single mum is no picnic. You'll get no respite. You'll be on demand 24/7."

"I can handle that. I'll do anything for my—our child."

"I'm sure you will." He reached out to touch the top of her hand. "But there is only my mother and me, and she is, well, outmoded in her outlook on love and marriage. She wouldn't understand you having my baby and me not marrying you. Me not standing up to my responsibilities."

"You could explain that we don't love each other."

"Hell, Honey, that's so lame, and not a reasonable excuse, not in my mother's eyes. She'd say, we loved each other enough to make a life, and now we're both responsible for that life. To take care and protect our child." He stared at his hands. "There's only you and your father, isn't there?"

Miserable, she nodded. "Yes."

"How would he take you having a baby and not being married?"

"He'd be delighted about the baby," she said. Her shoulders slumped. "He wouldn't like it for me."

"I didn't think he would. So the right thing for all is for us to marry."

"Right thing?" she exploded. "You have such a nasty way of putting things."

He stirred in his chair. "Hey, look, this isn't my idea of fun."

"You think I want to be tied to you, think again, mister."

"Married to you? Why it'd be simpler and saner to marry Medusa. All I need with her is a blindfold. With you I'd need the strength of Hercules double-folded."

"And you think I'm drooling at the corners of my mouth at the thought of being tied to you?" Charli snapped. "Get real. And don't think for one moment that I'm going to consider this ridiculous proposal. I have no intention of marrying you or anyone for that matter. I could think of nothing worse. You're rude, insufferable, and utterly arrogant. I'd rather marry a Martian with a horn for a head than marry you."

"Please be quiet for at least a minute. Ever since I've met you, you've had something to say and most of it never made any sense."

Charli shook her head. "This is ridiculous. I can't believe I'd—you'd—"

"Shut up," he yelled and then drew in a deep breath. "Sorry about the yelling. Our baby needs a daddy. And, at this time in your life, you need protection. I can offer both. We could make a go of this if we remain cool and logical."

"I agree the baby needs a father, it's marrying you that sticks in my neck."

"I'd never intended getting married again. Once, believe me, was truly enough. Have you got any romantic ideas about love and marriage?"

Yes, I have. I want someone who'll court me until I fall for him and he falls in love with me. I want someone who'll love me forever. We'll eat popcorn and potato chips watching television, I want dogs and cats and fish in a bowl and I want us to go bowling every Friday night. And when the kids are asleep in bed, I want to be with him in front of a roaring fire and make love. "No."

"Good, good. Let's look at this logically—."

Only the facts, ma'am. "Logic is so far better a word than romantic."

"What?"

"I want my job back as CE." She studied her fingernails.

"What? No way."

"Then no deal." She stood.

He waved her back to her seat. "If I agree then you'll marry me?"

Then, before she could control the words, she said, "You don't love me."

"Now you're being childish. Love doesn't enter the equation. This marriage will work out because it lacks love. Don't you see? Can't you understand? There's no pretense about love. This is an arrangement for both business and—"

"You were going to say pleasure," she cut in.

"You'd be hard to resist; you're a beautiful woman."

"That's made my day."

"Look, I'm only trying to help make the situation bearable."

"Bearable? Hell, you have a way with words. A nasty way."

His eyes flashed sparks of chipped emeralds, but his voice was passive when he spoke. "And you're Miss Sweetness and Light, I suppose, who wouldn't hurt a fly?"

She sprung out of her chair, her fingers spread, her nails flashing. "Why you—you rat."

He followed suit, almost rushing around the table to stand in front of her. "That's what you want to hear, isn't it? That makes you feel virtuous about the whole affair. The poor innocent maiden forced to marry the wicket tyrant. Well, if that's what it takes to get you to marry me, okay, I can live with that."

He towered over her and the sheer nearness of him was suffocating. Her hand flew to her throat, determined not to allow her senses to reel under his potency. From the moment she'd met him, Will had projected this power over her, made her head spin along with her heart.

She hoped her stare would turn him to stone as she said haughtily. "What will we tell everyone at work?"

"That we're getting married."

"They'll be shocked, and that's putting it mildly."

He shrugged. "It's none of their business. We'll be the talk of the office for a week or two and then we'll be old news."

"I don't want them knowing about the baby."

"What does it matter who knows?"

She bristled at his insensitivity. "If they know, *Will*, they'll know we had to get married and not for love."

His eyes softened. "That would hurt?"

Her turn to shrug. *Yes, it hurts because I want you to love me.* What? Where did that come from? Will love her? This was a straight-out shotgun wedding and she was a woman who could handle anything that came her way and come out smelling of roses. Couldn't she? "Stupid pride I guess. I'd like them to think we're in love."

He reached over and touched her hand. She drew back as if she'd been burned. They remained silent until Will said. "Is that all your conditions?"

"Yes."

"And if I agree, you'll marry me?"

"Yes, but don't expect me to sleep with you. That's asking too much."

He grinned. "Aww, shucks," he said.

"And I don't want you flaunting your women in front of me. I hope you can remain chaste until after the baby's born?"

"You think I'm a sex addict?"

"Yes, as a matter of fact, I do."

"A year's a long time without sex."

"Take up knitting. It'll keep your hands occupied."

"It's not my hands I'm worried about."

Despite his quip, he seemed dejected but it could have been the moonlight streaming through the window and casting his face in shadow. "Our parents need to know that we're getting married. That's a given, we don't have to tell them about the baby until much later."

"Are we going to say it's a premature birth?"

He frowned. "They won't care once they have their grandchild in their arms."

"That's so true." She raked a hand back through her hair and exhaled.

She cursed herself for her brusqueness. They were in this situation together. She knew what she was getting into and so did Will. So why the ravished maiden act every time he reminded her of the reason they were marrying? Because it hurt so damn much, that's why.

Chapter Nine

Getting to know you. Walks in the rain. Holding hands. Kissing.

Charli was in the living room in an old tracksuit lying on the floor following exercises from her workout pregnancy tape. She liked the tape as loud as she could reasonably have it. It saved her mind from being distracted by any other sound that filtered through her window from the street outside.

She was calmer today. The incredible pressure and tension of the past days had gone and she was determined to remain this way; allowing nothing or no one to alter this feeling of semi-peace.

Following the tape, Charli lay on her back with her knees bent. Inhaled through her nose and tightened her stomach and buttock muscles. Flattened the small of her back against the floor and allowed her pelvis to tilt upward.

His head, poking through the open window, loomed down at her from between her stretched legs. Startled, she said, "Please go away. You're ruining my concentration."

"My concentration's lapsing too."

She jumped to her feet and ran her hands down the sides of her pants. He gave her a brief scrutiny. If he made any crack about what she was wearing she'd throw the nearest thing she could grab at him. "Ever heard of knocking?"

"I rang your doorbell for a good two minutes. Just going to give up when I saw this window open."

"So you poke your head through and scare me half to death?"

"It was an open invitation to me and every thief within a mile radius. Besides, I have certain privileges."

"How come?"

"Goes with rank." He grinned and with supreme effort, she controlled her mouth from responding. "Open the front door."

He winked when she opened the door. "Hi, just passing by, saw your lights on and thought hey, she might give me a cup of coffee."

"Well, you thought wrong." She moved back into the living room, picked up a towel and wiped her face and arms.

He laughed softly and took the towel from her and wiped the back of her neck and shoulders. She swung angrily away from him, grabbing the towel. "I don't need a nursemaid, thanks, Will. I'm perfectly capable of dry toweling my body."

"And it was giving me such pleasure."

She flicked her hair. "Too bad." She sniffed.

"Why are you always so angry?"

"I'm not angry, it's just that you make me feel—"

He moved in closer. "Sexy?"

"Queasy."

"Is that a nice word for nauseated?"

She worried her bottom lip. She didn't actually want to hurt him by acerbic retorts, but she wanted to put him in his rightful place, wherever that may be and it was true he did make her feel uneasy, a sort of seasickness sensation she always got when he was around her.

She'd nothing to fear from Will Knight. He didn't affect her in any way except maybe her libido.

She could handle him. The situation. Why she could handle anything that came her way with both hands tied behind her back.

She lusted after Will. He was, except for his arrogance and stubborn streak, a gorgeous man. And he turned her on hot and willing. It'd been a long time since a man had had that power over her. Who was she kidding? She'd never known a man who had tingled as much as her big toe. When Will kissed her, she'd actually heard bells. Now, that had to mean something, didn't it?

Holy crap. She didn't want his kisses to mean anything to her. She didn't want this man with an ego the size of Mount Everest to affect her in the slightest way.

A conundrum. She'd wanted him as much as he'd wanted her. So what had been the problem? Why had she sent him packing and crept back into her lonely bed like a nun on retreat?

It didn't make sense.

It must be that she was confused. Yes, that was it; total confusion. He was harassing her about marriage and, and— she mentally sighed—and every other damn thing she'd always wanted in her life.

It couldn't be love. Love didn't just happen. It was an over-the-years-and-took-patience-and-understanding type of occurrence. It was courtship, deepening affection, love, and marriage.

What was happening now? She was caught up in a web of excitement like some helpless fly and Will the spider coming to eat her. Hmm.

She changed the subject completely. "I'm about to have a coffee, want some?"

He nodded, and followed her into the kitchen. She grabbed the percolator and filled it with water.

He slumped onto a chair. "My mother wants to meet you. We're invited for dinner next Saturday."

She jerked. Water splashed over her hand and arms. With trembling fingers, she scooped coffee into the filter and put the coffee on to percolate. She slumped into a chair opposite him. She stretched out her feet and stared dejectedly at her toes. "Does—" she swallowed, "Does your mother know about us already?"

"She does."

His confirmation in those two controlled words had her rising out of her chair, only to find he had risen as well. He moved to stand directly in front of her.

Charli was horrified. "How could you tell her so soon? I wasn't ready. I need time to gather my thoughts. I have to think about things. This is too fast." She grabbed his sweater and shook him. "You've got to give me time."

He prized free her fear-stricken fingers. "Hey, go easy. You're bending the wool."

She curled her fingers. "How about I bend your neck?"

"Come on, Honey. She had to know some time."

Charli groaned inwardly. The situation was going from bad to worse; fast. "Was she surprised?"

"You could say that."

"Was she pleased?"

"It's difficult to tell."

"Then she was displeased?"

"I wouldn't say that."

"Then what would you say?"

"I'd say she was shocked."

"Oh, God."

Charli's head was swimming. To think that he'd gone and told his mother when she was still planning the right words as to how she could break the news to her father. Nothing seemed to faze this man. He was accepting their marriage as if it was an everyday event, and yet she knew how hurt he was over his wife's desertion. The pain of grief and humiliation he'd suffered. He must have taken a vow never to trust his heart to another woman, and who could blame him?

And now he was marrying her to give his child his name so no fingers could ever be pointed at him. Will couldn't be a long-distance daddy, she knew this. He'd want to share and care with him. To protect and love him as a father should. *What about me? I need love too.*

A cloud of despondency settled around her head. Her mind wandered and her eyes fluttered closed...

I'm standing tall, the light from yonder window curling a golden halo around my head. I fold my arms across my breast and intone, "I'll never sacrifice my honor. I reject the idea of marrying for anything less than love."

Will flings himself at my feet picking up the hem of my dress and kissing it fervently, says, "But it is love, my Honey. I love you more than anything in the entire world." Standing, he scoops me into his arms and presses his hot mouth against my eager own. My blood heats as every nerve in my body responds. I want him desperately. I want him inside me. Only Will can satisfy this urgent need.

Bells sound.

Her eyes flew wide open. *Oh my God, I'm in love with William Knight.*

She wasn't marrying Will to appease their parents, or even her wonderful job back at Knight Books. She wanted Will. This was worse than anything she could ever imagine. She'd have to fight this feeling of love for him because it would cause her more grief than she'd ever known. In love with a man who would never, could never love her back.

"Hell-lo-o, anyone home?"

"What?"

"You were picking daisies again. What I said was, don't go making mountains out of molehills; allowing that crazy imagination of yours to go riot."

"I shall make whatever I want out of whatever I want." She sniffed. "And my imagination is as normal as anyone's, thanks very much."

He laughed. "I've never known a woman like you," he said.

Miffed, she straightened. "Is this some sort of compliment, Will, or should I expect the rug ripped out from under me, yet again?"

He reached over and touched her hair, running his fingers down the side of her face. Power surge. If only she didn't have this fantastic desire for Will. Every time he touched her she melted. She had to keep reminding herself what this marriage was all about. There was no love involved. There never would be.

Yet even knowing that, each time she was with him her feelings for him deepened. How could she possibly live with him in the same house and remain sane.

Her mantra for the week; *I will not love Will. I will not love Will.*

She moved to the cupboard, took down mugs and filled them with coffee. "Milk and sugar?"

"Three."

She gawked. "Three sugars?"

"I've got a sugar fixation." He patted his top pocket. "Always got a chocolate bar on me."

"That's being prepared, if you get lost in the bush, that is." She handed him his coffee and resumed her seat. He followed suit. "And she wants to meet me?"

"Yep, she sure does. What's wrong with that? Every mother wants to meet the woman her son plans to marry." He studied her face. "When do you think you'll tell your father?"

Charli gasped weakly. Telling her father about her impending marriage wasn't her idea of a good time. Whatever would he think? Pain filled her heart. He wouldn't care one way or the other. As far as her father was concerned, Charli could marry whom she pleased. He no longer cared if she was happy or sad. The day her mother died she had lost both her parents. How could she explain this to Will?

"My father?" she said, vaguely seeking time to find the right answer to give Will.

"Yeah, the man you grew up with. Remember him?"

"Don't be insulting."

He sighed. "Look, Honey. We're getting married. There's family involved. We have to tell our parents. We have to tell your father." He lowered his head and peered into her eyes. She blinked. "Are you grasping any of this?"

"It's too soon," she argued.

"Tonight, tomorrow, or next week, the meeting is inevitable so why put it off? You're not on trial; this is just a meeting between you and my mother."

"She'll expect something better than me," she pouted.

"What the hell?" he said. "What are you prattling on about now?"

"The poor secretary marrying the rich boss. The old, old story. Your mother will think I've trapped you somehow into marriage."

He raised an eyebrow. "For one thing you aren't my secretary and another is you're not smart enough to trap me."

"You are unforgivably insulting."

"There are two ways we can go about this thing," Will was saying. "We can tell our parents the truth and break their hearts, or we can pretend we love each other. The choice is yours, but whatever you choose, whichever way you go, the ending is still the same."

Fear struck deep within her; Will was right, whatever happened there was no getting out of it.

Chapter Ten

A gentleman should tip his hat when meeting a lady on the street.

Charli changed for the fifth time, throwing the discarded dress on top of the others, which were lying in crumpled mess across the bed.

She didn't know what to wear. This wasn't a casual outing; she was to meet William's mother and quite frankly, she was scared witless.

She stared vacantly into her wardrobe; something not too elaborate yet sophisticated. She flicked through her clothes, wishing she'd followed her first instinct and bought something new. Sighing deeply, she spun away from the wardrobe and fell across the bed on top of her discarded clothes and stared at the ceiling.

It had taken her several attempts to telephone her father and after rehearsing over and over in her mind what she would say to him, she'd finally dialed his number.

His elation at her news thrilled her and he'd sounded like the father she'd known before her mother had died, eager, laughing, joking with her, then seriously telling her how pleased he was for her that she'd found someone who loved her and when could he meet him? It was nearly worth it to marry Will to make her father this happy.

She was marrying a man who didn't love her. All her life she'd dreamt of courting, love, and marriage, in that order. Now it was marriage, no love, and certainly no courting.

Okay, what she'd do was throw herself into Knight Books. She had some wonderful ideas on how to improve the company. She'd work fourteen hours a day, come home so exhausted that she'd collapse into bed and sleep the night away until it was time to return to work the next morning. She'd work weekends as well. Nose to the grindstone was her middle name from now on. Good plan.

And she thought that Will would approve. His goal was to make Knight Books the best publishing house in Australia. Well, that was her goal too. At work, they would be side by side making snap decisions, enjoying every moment of working together. It was at home, at night that worried her.

Because loving him hurt.

Tears fell down her cheeks. A sensation not unlike little girl lost assailed her. Why was she so upset? She was going into this marriage with eyes wide open. Will had never lied to her. He didn't love her nor would he ever love her.

"And I don't love him," she tested the lie, brushing the tears away with the back of her hand.

Chastising herself for wallowing in self-pity, she plucked a tissue from the box on the dressing table and loudly blew her nose. Tossing the tissue into the wastepaper basket, she resumed searching through the wardrobe.

At last, she decided on a claret and black paisley velour top, rich with color and pattern, with a cocoa brown skirt in an easy flow of suede-touch polyester. Softly pleated with extra length that covered the top of her brown suede boots.

Desperate to look as sophisticated as possible, she pinned her hair into a chignon on the top of her head. Her hair refused to obey and kept falling loose of its combs. Eventually she gave up and allowed her hair to cascade in curling waves to her shoulders.

Will arrived five minutes early. She'd been ready for him long before he'd arrived. He looked different today dressed as he was in dark slacks and lightweight sea green sweater that brought out the vividness of his eyes. He left her breathless.

A flicker of appreciation shone in his eyes, as he looked her up and down. "You look lovely," he said.

Charli felt a wash of pleasure at his compliment. She tried telling herself that she didn't give a damn if he liked what she wore or not. But that simply wasn't true. She cared deeply what he thought of her.

She was tumbling headlong into an abyss. She'd lost control of her senses. She could blame it on his impish smile, his smoldering looks, and seductive voice.

She could handle the situation between her and Will, and marrying him wasn't scaring the living daylights out of her. She could imagine that their marriage was one of love. That Will had fallen in love with her. All he cared about was making her his wife and loving her for the rest of his life.

She could say that, but it wasn't true, and all the wishing and hoping wouldn't make it so.

And even if she wanted out of the marriage it was too late. Their parents knew. The people at work knew. And she wanted security for her baby. She wanted him to grow up strong and proud in the knowledge that his parents loved him above all else.

It'll be all right, she assured herself as Will followed her inside. She collected her handbag and coat. He came silently behind her. She gasped as his fingers touched her shoulders causing her to stop. He fastened a necklace around her neck. She fingered a string of exquisite natural pearls and spun around to face him. "I couldn't possibly accept these."

"Don't deny me giving you a small gift."

"A small gift, yes, but these most have cost a fortune."

"They match your skin," he said. "Creamy, soft, and the color of ivory."

He spun her brain like a spinning top. He came on hot and cold in a matter of seconds. She couldn't work out what was going on behind those indescribable eyes. Who was the real Will

Knight? The warm and totally inviting man that stood before her now or the arrogant and compelling man that bent her to his will? If only she didn't have this eerie fascination for him. He was such a mystery to her and one she longed to solve.

He placed his arm around her waist moving her toward the door. "My mother is a woman one doesn't keep waiting," he said.

They drove in relative silence until they reached Portsea. Charli gazed in admiration at the beautiful scenery, which manifested before her eyes in blue seas, limestone cliffs, and thunderous surf. Victoria's summer social capital. Mansions and weekend cottages flourished, some of them more than a century old.

William steered the car through the wrought iron gates to the main house. Were it not for the ti-trees, the gums, and the vivid blue sky, Charli would have imagined she was in a European resort. To the left of the house was a luxurious glittering swimming pool, looking placid and invitingly blue in the late afternoon sun.

His mother's home was a two-story brick mansion. Timber gable ends, balustrades, shingles, eaves, and window frames were white with natural-colored brickwork.

"Will, it's lovely," Charli enthused.

He braked in front of the house, alighted from the car, and moved around to open the door for her. He ushered her inside the house.

The room they entered was obviously the sitting room. The walls were pale blue, the deeper, true turquoise chairs and sofas, the creamy beige carpet. She admired the feature brick wall in which a fireplace was set. The room was on a split-level. There was a small flight of stairs and through an arched opening, there was the library.

A tall, very elegant, and slightly overweight woman rose to greet them. She had impeccable taste like Audrey Hepburn or Lauren Bacall, dressed in a Gabrielle jacket in black tweed, Tina pearl muted snakeskin ballet shoes, and a sunray pleat maxi-skirt.

She oozed sophistication and confidence. Charli felt a flash of admiration for her taste in clothes alone.

"William, my son," she enthused, like she hadn't seen him for ten years. She placed a soft kiss on her son's cheek. "And this must be—?" She arched a delicately plucked eyebrow.

Will placed his hand in the small of Charli's back and nudged her gently toward his mother. "Honey, this is my mother, Ester Knight. Mother, this is Charli Honey."

There was a momentary silence as the older woman drank her in. On parade? Should she stand at attention and salute? Or perhaps just lower her head until the inspection was over.

Why was she thinking such bitchy thoughts? She didn't know Ester Knight. Perhaps she was a kind and generous woman. Perhaps she'd like her instantly and they would become bosom pals. Perhaps pigs would indeed one day fly.

"So you are the girl my son wants to marry." Statement not question.

"Yes," Charli muttered. "I am she. The one he wants to marry." Had she lost her power of speech? Why was she muttering like a bag lady rummaging through a trash bin? And was that a look of utter disappointment, maybe bordering on disgust on Ester Knight's face? *Oh my God, she doesn't like me.* "I'm so pleased to meet you, Mrs. Knight."

"Please call me Ester."

"Ester."

"We must have an engagement party."

"What?" both Charli and Will said.

"You cannot get married without first making an announcement. It isn't done." She held up one hand at their stuttering protests. "What are your plans? Please tell me."

"We want to get married and as soon as possible," Charli said. "No fuss or bother. Just a quick wedding and that's that."

"Why the haste? Surely, you've only just met." Her eyes traveled down to Charli's tummy. Charli immediately placed her hand over the offending space and held her breath. Does she suspect? And if Ester challenges her, what should she say?

Charli felt immediate relief when Ester said, "Now no more talk of rushing things. I need to meet your parents and you and your parents will meet Will's family. Does your mother require any help with the wedding plans?"

"My mother is dead."

"Oh, I'm sorry. Forgive me, I had no idea. Have you anyone who can help you with the arrangements?"

"Nobody."

"Wonderful. Then I'll go immediately into action. It's been my burning ambition to arrange a wedding—not just any old person's wedding, but my son's. Not that I expected him to find an orphan just to please me," she gushed and Charli's head whirled. "But seeing he has, well, isn't it exciting. I know this great little wedding planner. She did my cousin's daughter's wedding and it was superb. There's so much to be done, but that will never daunt me. I look on it as a challenge. The engagement shall be a small do, to be held here at my home."

Could she excuse herself? Say she had a migraine and needed fresh air or that she just remembered she'd left the gas on at home. Charli wasn't sure what she'd expected from the meeting with Will's mother. A cup of tea and buttered scones? Will talk?

"I'll do everything necessary so you don't have to worry your pretty little head."

"Mum, we didn't want too much fuss. A simple wedding with a civil service." Will shook his head slightly. "No fuss, please, Mum," he repeated. "We were thinking Registry Office or in a park with just family and a few close friends."

Her face actually drained of color, her eyes widened until Charli thought they would pop from their sockets. "My dear God, William, did I hear you correctly? Registry Office? A-a-"

She swallowed noticeably. "Park? With strangers staring on and birds pooping through the dangling leaves? I think not. Oh, no, I think not for my son."

Will looked flummoxed. "Mum, please, I beg you. We want a simple, easy wedding. Okay, we'll take the engagement party if that's what you want, but we're firm-footed about the wedding." He turned to Charli. "Aren't we, Honey?"

"Oh, um, yes, our feet are pretty firm."

She was a mess. An inept crazy woman who couldn't string a sentence together. Ester Knight's words raced around her brain. The whole situation was completely out of control. She knew Will was trying to take control but he was floundering too. His mother was, to say the least, a strong and determined woman. So be it.

"Darling, I assure you it will be a simple wedding and with a civil service." She smiled benevolently. "It's my wedding gift to you both."

There was no escape. How could they refuse his mother's gift? Oh my God, she'd have to walk down the aisle into her not so loving husband's arms with everyone looking on dewy-eyed.

Not for this little black duck. There had to be an escape clause somewhere.

In her mind's eye, she saw Will placing a ladder at her window, her climbing down, and them rushing off to Tasmania, heck no, make that Las Vegas, much more romantic. He might even take her to Hollywood. She was a sucker for the stars and a tour of their houses would be high on her list of things to do in movieland.

"Honey!"

She blinked. "What?"

"You're woolgathering again. Mum was asking you a question."

"Sorry, Ester. You were saying?"

"Is your name a derivative?"

"Excuse me?" Charli said.

"Your name? Is it short for Charlotte, or Charlene or something in that vein?"

Something tight and unwelcomed squeezed Charli's heart. Her first assumption was right—Ester didn't like her. "It's just Charli."

"Pity. Charli will appear so—so gauche on the invitations."

Will interjected. "She can't change her name to suit the invitations, mother," he said and his eyes twinkled with humor.

He was enjoying this now. His mother was behaving exactly as he expected her to. Why hadn't he warned her? And how dare he let his mother insult her name.

"Come, sit down here on the settee with me," Ester said patting the space beside her. Charli, like an obedient child, did as she was bid. Where was her stamina, her chutzpah she was so proud of?

Ester Knight leaned forward in her chair and fingered Charli's hair. "Is this a dye?"

"No." Charli denied hotly.

"This is really the color of your hair. It's so red."

"That's because it is red."

Ester crossed her arms across her ample bosom. "It will look radiant against white."

"White?"

"Your bridal dress, Charlene."

"Charli," Charli corrected.

"Whatever. Your magnificent dress that—" At this point Ester Knight tilted back her head, crossed her hands over her breasts and fluttered her eyelids closed. "If I close my eyes I can see you, with your veil billowing out behind you as you float majestically down the aisle. Is your father tall?"

"Pardon me?"

"Your father, is he tall?"

"He's around five foot ten or eleven, I suppose," Charli stammered.

"Couldn't be more perfect. I think there's nothing more distasteful than a bride with a short father. It doesn't gel, so to speak."

Charli didn't answer because she had no idea how to respond. She threw a pleading glance at Will. He raised his shoulders slightly, sent her a pitying look but remained silent.

In a ping of enlightenment, Charli realized that her earlier assumption about Ester not liking her was wrong. In fact Will's mother didn't care about her one way or the other, she was treating Charli the same as she'd treat a cleaning woman applying for a job in Ester's home, wanting to know the general things. Did the woman drink? Was she reliable? Any moment Ester Knight would ask her for a character reference. This was so damn awful.

"Who will you choose for bridesmaids, Charlene?"

Oh, God let this all be a bad dream. "I hadn't thought about bridesmaids. And my name is *Charli*."

"Charli, yes of course, how remiss of me." Her apology was vague. "Are you content to leave it to me? Would you like that, dear?"

"Yes, I suppose so," she said. "Except for one thing, Ester?"

Ester Knight drew herself erect. "And that is?"

"The flowers are my father's prerogative? He's a master gardener and his flowers are the envy of Rich River."

Ester Knight raised an arched eyebrow. "Rich—?"

"Rich River, where my father lives. Where I was born." She didn't want any of this, and she wondered if maybe she should run for her dad's farm and hide in the cow shed. Get a grip, for God's sake.

So there was to be an engagement party, she could handle that. And as for the wedding, hadn't she always dreamed of a white wedding, thrown rice, a honeymoon with the man she loved. Ah, there was the operative word 'love.' *Love is a many splendored thing; love conquered all; the power of love*, etcetera, etcetera.

"But I know this most divine little florist who makes—"

Charli stood, her fists clenched. "No, Ester, I insist that my father handles the flowers. You can do everything else you wish but the flowers belong to my side of the family and that's that."

"Well, I never," Ester Knight said. "A temper to match the hair." She threw a glance toward her son. "William, I do believe you've met your match. Be a good boy and break open a bottle of champagne. We'll toast the engagement."

*

Will exploded into laughter as soon as they got into the car to go back to the city.

Charli threw him a resentful look. "I don't see what's so blasted funny."

"My mother and the wedding. Come on, Charli, you have to admit it was hilarious."

"I'm pleased you found amusement in my embarrassment. Your mother won't be satisfied until she arranges a wedding that will equal if not better a royal's."

"Most probably," he said.

"And why didn't you help me? Surely you don't want this farce any more than I do. It's bad enough we're getting married without all this false trimming."

"Help you and spoil my afternoon's entertainment? Don't think so."

"Your mother's very determined." She shot him a sideward glance. "You're very much alike."

"Ouch. That hurt. I pride myself that I take after my father."

She placed her head back on the headrest. "She doesn't like me," she said quietly.

"Who?"

"Your mother."

"She likes to organize events, it's just her way."

She sat bolt upright. "Will, your mother couldn't even remember my name and she detested the color of my hair."

"She was excited that's all."

"No, she wasn't. She was disappointed, and she's sorry that you're not marrying the society girl she thinks you should marry."

"Stop it, Honey."

"She thinks I'm not good enough for you."

He jammed on the brakes and she flung forward in her seat hearing the resounding snap of the safety belt holding her securely in place. He looked at her and she could see the anger flare in his eyes.

"I'm sorry, I didn't mean to sound trite. I didn't know how else to say it."

The anger died at her words and he spoke gently to her. "Don't worry about anything. It'll all work out. I promise you."

He put the car into gear and sped off down the highway.

It was all right for him to say everything would work out. How could anything be all right when they didn't love each other and his mother disliked her?

She could see the invitations now, Mrs. Ester Knight requests the pleasure of...to witness the marriage of her only son William Knight to Charlene—Charlotte—what's-her-name Honey.

The next time she met his mother she'd most likely stare blankly at her and say, *now, William, which little friend of yours is this?* Or something as equally cruel.

These people were out of her realm. They belonged to a world that Charli had never entered. She couldn't keep up with them and she didn't want to try. She didn't want to live in a big marble and glass house on the top of a hill overlooking the city. She wanted her career for sure, but she wanted to fit it in around a man who loved her, a dog and a cat, six kids, and a mortgage that would choke a horse. She wanted to go shopping on a Thursday night with her husband and buy doughnuts and ice cream. Go to the movies on a Saturday night after a counter meal at the local pub, washed down with a glass of icy cold beer. She wanted holidays they'd saved all year for.

Okay, so it wasn't to be. She'd made her bed and now she had to lie in it. She glanced at Will's profile. Alone!

Charli wanted love. She wanted to love her husband and know, with a quiet certainty, that he loved her more than anything else in life.

Charli closed her eyes; tears burned.

Chapter Eleven

Traditionally it has been perceived that it is the role of a male to actively "court" or "woo" the female, thus encouraging her to understand him and her receptiveness to a proposal of marriage.

Their wedding announcement took everyone by surprise. Charli smiled broadly recalling the astonished expression on Judy's face when she had told her she was marrying the boss. "I knew he'd do the right thing by the baby, but marriage? You don't even like him."

"I saw his good side."

"For God's sake, Charli, this is crazy. You can't detest a man and then marry him a few days later."

"Of course you can."

"You'd never have money problems anymore. He'd've looked after you and the baby financially. So why tie the knot?"

"We want the best for our baby. And there are our parents to consider. Dad's depressed enough as it is without me being pregnant and no husband in sight. I don't think he could take that. He's very old school."

"But marriage without love. It won't work."

"I don't know. What about all those Katherine Hepburn and Spencer Tracy movies? They always started off disliking each other and getting married and then falling in love."

Judy sighed. "I give up."

The news had spread rapidly throughout the office until even the tea-lady threw her a rather lurid wink. For the first time in her life, Charli was the center of attention and she didn't like it.

She had to get her private affairs in order. There was her apartment to consider and after deep deliberation, she decided to sell it and invest the money. She also sold most of the furniture, only keeping a few pieces that had belonged to her mother and with which she'd never part.

Judy had approached her and suggested lunch with the girls from the office. Just what the doctor ordered, Charli thought, an enjoyable hens' afternoon.

The girls had all chipped in and brought her a miniature weeping fig tree planted in an opaque, blue-green ceramic pot.

She'd expected a few snide remarks, maybe a snigger or two, but she couldn't have been more wrong. The girls were genuinely excited for her, wishing her happiness and love forever.

She glanced over at the weeping fig tree standing majestically in the corner of her bedroom. She'd plant it in the garden when she was settled in with Will.

She knew Knight Books owned a penthouse suite at one of the major city hotels and that Will stayed at his uncle's house in Kew. This was where they would live after their marriage.

He'd taken her there last Sunday. His house was on a street that was a beautiful leafy tunnel, winding around a steep hillside, with only patches of sun filtering down to the road. There were Japanese cherry trees and tall, masterful gums.

Entry to the house was through a solid gate to a courtyard. He'd taken her on a grand tour. After all, he'd said to her, this was to be her home.

Dining, living, kitchen, laundry and bathrooms were on the ground floor, which was white marble throughout. The wide balcony off the living room was also marble. Huge sliding glass doors gave unhindered views over the city proper. Five double bedrooms with their own large balconies were on the second floor.

It had been awe-inspiring to say the least. She glanced again at her plant.

"Don't worry, little fig tree. I'll find a great spot for you among all those exotic plants, I promise you. Just as I have to find my own spot among Will's exotic friends."

Chapter Twelve

The ring is worn on the fourth finger of the left hand based upon a Grecian fable that the artery from that finger flows directly to the heart.

Will never gave her an engagement ring. He had no idea how to court a woman, and Charli had to admit that it hurt. Then she chided herself for her romanticism. When would she grow up and face the truth of their situation. It was a done deal. A handshake and a tap on the side of the nose.

She admired herself in the mirror. A strapless party dress of white chiffon that swirled around her legs at every movement, complete with a black satin sash. And in a mad moment she'd bought a pair of corsage strappy black sandals. Expensive, but she'd fallen in love with them at first sight.

A knock on her bedroom door had her saying, "Come in, Dad. I'm dressed and armed."

He was laughing when he entered the room. "You look lovely, darling."

"Thanks, Dad."

"I'm looking forward to meeting Will and his family."

Will, on his mother's insistence, was helping her with last-minute preparations and greeting guests. He'd wanted to pick them up from her flat but she'd protested. As they were all staying the night at Ester's it would be simpler to get a taxi and Will could drive them home in the morning. Still it was nice that he'd offered and showed he did have a little sensitivity where she was concerned.

"I've only just met his mother, and believe me, Dad, you're in for a treat."

"Nice lady?"

"Yes, of course, but she's—um, well she likes things orderly and she likes to be in charge."

He smiled. "So did your mum. She ran our life together with an iron rod. "

"I don't remember Mum being like that. She was soft, gentle, and loving."

"Yeah, she was that, but she was a strong, determined lady too." He nodded his head. "Just like you, Charli. You're the living image of your mum."

This was the first time her dad had ever suggested such a thing and it thrilled her to think he thought her like Mum. And now, when she really thought about it, their lives had crashed down upon them when her mum had died. She had been stalwart; the strength that kept the family together. And it came to Charli that women were the *rulers of the earth* and that behind every great man was a woman pushing him every inch of the way.

It strengthened her and she knew that she could handle Will Knight with one hand planted in a cement block and the other knitting him socks.

Charli's spirits lightened and she suddenly was looking forward to the party and, like her dad, meeting Will's family and friends.

A horn tooted. "That'll be the taxi," her dad said. He offered his arm, "Shall I escort you downstairs, m'lady?"

Charli gave a tiny bow. "That would be delightful, m'lord."

*

Even though they'd had left early wanting to be there before guests arrived, the party seemed to be in full swing when Charli and her dad arrived.

Will greeted them with a light kiss on Charli's cheek and a warm handshake for her dad.

"Dad, this is William Knight. Will, my father, Steve Honey."

"So pleased to meet you at last, Steve." The men shook hands.

As Will led them into a large room that had been set up for the party, he said, "You look absolutely magnificent. White's your color—you should wear it more often."

She laughed, delighted at his compliment and feeling more in control, more feminine by the minute.

People were chatting and laughing. In one corner, a pianist was tinkling out mood music. At the back was a long table covered in a lace cloth, behind which stood a black-and-white clad man, presumably the drink waiter.

"Like a drink, Steve?"

"Cold beer would go down well, thanks, Will."

"Champagne cocktail, Honey? Mum's specialty guaranteed to curl your hair with one sip. Or in your case straighten it."

She laughed. "I've always fancied my hair hanging long and straight, but I prefer an orange juice."

"Your hair is perfect as it is," Will said, and she couldn't control the blush that crept into her cheeks. Was that compliment for her father's benefit? Of course it was. Will wanted their parents to believe they were deeply in love. He couldn't have said anything less to her, now could he?

Will left them to get the drinks. "Who's the lady in the green dress with all the feathers and diamonds?"

"That's Ester, Will's mother."

"Nice stamp of a woman. Introduce me."

His face had more animation in it that she'd seen for a long time. Why, he was almost salivating. "Dad, you behave."

It pleased her that her dad was healing. This was the first time he'd shown interest in another woman since her mother had died. No, retract that, he'd never shown interest in any other woman but her mother, and now, his eyes were twinkling over Ester Knight. A woman Charli thought her father would well steer clear of. Yet he saw something in Will's mum that she hadn't.

She looked over at Ester. Could it be that she was warmer than Charli had thought? What was that saying, never judge on first impressions?

They walked over to where Ester was talking with a tall, thin man. "Ester, excuse me for interrupting, but I'd like you to meet my father."

Ester turned and when her eyes landed on Steve, her mouth broke into a wide grin. *My God, is this a mutual admiration society? Is she having a—I hate to use the word sexual—is she having a friendly reaction to my dad?*

"Dad, this is Will's mother, Ester Knight. Ester, my father, Steve Honey."

Ester held out a long white hand. "So pleased to meet you, Steven," she almost gushed the words. "We've got so much to talk about. You know, the wedding, the guest list, and the flowers, which I believe you'll be handling and I'm sure in a most delightful manner. Can you give me a few minutes, say, after everyone has left? We could have a cocoa before bed." She smiled. "Or maybe something stronger."

Her father actually bowed. What's going on here? "I'd be delighted," he said.

"And this is my brother, Duncan Meadows, Duncan, Steven Honey and his daughter, Will's fiancé, Charli." And so the introductions went on until Charli's head was swirling trying to place names to faces.

It was a good party, and everyone was enjoying themselves when a little bell sounded and Ester's strong voice echoed across the sea of sound. "Time for toasts," she said. "And I believe William wants to be first." She smiled indulgently at Will.

Will came to her side and took Charli's hand. He led her to the front of the table and looked down at her. If she didn't know better she'd say there was a warm look in his eyes, sort of like, well—love. Get real.

He took her hand, groped in his pants pocket and came out with a little black box. Her heart leaped in her chest. Was it? Could it be? Maybe it was a broach, or a pair of diamond earrings, which would be good, she reassured herself, and then braced for disappointment.

"Honey," Will said. "You have promised to be my wife and made me a very happy man."

Yeah, what fairy tale did that come from?

He lifted the lid and removed a ring that boasted diamonds and pearls. He slipped it on her finger, bent his gorgeous head and kissed her mouth. She wondered if she should say thank you, or return his kiss with all the passion she carried for him deep down inside her heart?

She gazed down at the ring and remembered reading somewhere that in the 1800s a diamond and pearl engagement ring was suggestive of a diamond tiara across the finger. She loved it.

She didn't want to think of the *if only's*. This was her night to imagine that this was real. Will's touch of tenderness. This beautiful ring on her finger. Here in this lovely room with all these lovely people who wanted to include her in their family, accept her, and love her. It was such a great night.

Then everyone was congratulating them. Kisses and hugs all around.

The night ended in such a warm glow that Charli practically floated to her room. She hopped into bed and fell asleep, her right hand clasped over Will's ring.

Chapter Thirteen

Be interested in all she does and always tell her how lovely she looks.
Be honest and she'll love you all the more for it.

Will insisted on seeing her father's farm. She tried to fob him off, as she couldn't understand the reason behind his insistence that he hadn't had time to really get to know her dad, but finally she'd given in and taken him to Rich River.

Between the two men, a kinship arose; as if there had always been a deeply rooted friendship that was both comfortable and easy. Her father proudly showed Will over the farm and Will behaved as if he'd never been in the country before.

"I've been lucky," Dad told Will. "I've got good revenues to sell my flowers. I've made a pretty comfortable life here in Rich River."

"A lot of work for one man," Will said.

"Not once you've got it all under control, and I have a couple of local men helping me out." He reached out to touch Charli's cheek. "Not like my kid here. Big knob in a publishing house. She sure is a clever girl."

"Take after you, Dad."

"Could do worse. And working together is great for a marriage. Why, your mum and me, we were together 24/7 and never once had more than a few angry words. Although she did go off shopping or to the movies once a week. To get me out of her hair, she'd say." He chuckled. "And I played a round of golf now and then. I think another secret to a good marriage is each having an interest to call one's own."

"You sure found the key, Dad. You and Mum had a perfect marriage."

"That we did, love. That we did." He stood and stretched. "You kids must be starving. I'll get lunch going."

Will stood. "Can I help you, Steve?"

"No, son, you sit and finish your beer. I like to potter about on my own."

Will sat back down and they watched Steve disappear inside the house. "I like your dad," he said. "He's a good bloke."

"And he likes you."

"Do you think so? I like to think he does like me."

She leaned over and touched his arm. "You're easy to like, Will." She grinned. "Sometimes."

"Why do you always have to qualify?"

"It's the meanness in me."

He leaned over and kissed her mouth. "Yeah, then I reckon I'll just have to mellow you out."

They drew apart as her dad emerged, juggling plates and cutlery. He cooked them a barbeque lunch of his specialty, sausages, fried onions and mushrooms, squashed into a big bun smothered with tomato sauce that dripped down your fingers.

Charli decided the day was exactly how she wanted it to be.

Being with the two men she loved more than anything else in the world.

*

That night the three of them sat on her father's well-worn veranda, Charli sipping an ice-cold glass of ginger beer, her dad and Will drinking beer from a can, the way her father had always drunk his beer for as long as she could remember.

After her father had retired for the evening, Charli and Will went for a walk along the well-trod paths of the Murray and sat near the river's edge throwing stones into the deep, dark water.

She was glad now that she'd taken Will to the farm. She'd wanted him to know her slice of life. Let him see how she'd been raised, and maybe he'd understand her uneasiness while around Ester Knight.

"Your father reminds me of my dad," Will said. "Down to earth, strong and dependable."

Surprised, she said, "What did your father do?"

"He built houses."

"He owned a construction company."

"No, he built houses. He loved to build." He gave a quiet laugh. "I know what you're thinking. How come my mother married a builder? Simple, she fell in love with him. He never changed and neither did she. My mother came from a moneyed family. Her father was a heart surgeon and her mother a renowned psychiatrist. The house in Portsea belonged to her parents."

"That's your family home."

"Nope. I was born in Warrandyte."

"But your mother seems so—"

"She likes to play lady of the manor." He shrugged. "So what? Besides me, that's all she's got." He stood and helped her to her feet. "My mother loved my father and when he died she was heartbroken for years. Her parents were killed in a car accident and I encouraged her to take over the house in Portsea. To give her substance. To give her a reason to live."

He threaded his arm through hers as they made their way back to her father's house. Charli said quietly, "I didn't know. Didn't understand."

They reached the veranda. He spun her around, clasping his arms around her waist. She stared up and in the moonlight his eyes sparkled. "Just be yourself, Honey. Don't change, whatever you do. That's all I ask."

His lips made a soft, embracing trail across her cheek to the lobe of her ear.

She brought her hands up to push him away but she might have been pushing a mountain so ineffectual were her efforts.

"Kiss me," he said. His hands moved to the small of her back, pressing her to him, bringing her mouth in contact with his. "Kiss me."

His eyes devoured her. Electricity sparked. His mouth covered hers and the world tilted. His mouth demanded. She responded. She was totally his.

He released her mouth. He claimed her mouth. He allowed the tip of his tongue to caress the inside of her mouth. Passion soared. Uncontrollable and fierce. Hot and powerful.

His hand clasped her breast, pressing the fullness. Her hands wound around his neck. The kiss would never end. He made to lift his head. She gave a small moan and traced his lips with her own. All-consuming heat. A need that must be fulfilled.

Her head fell back and his mouth trailed kisses down her throat. She could feel the heat of his mouth through the thick shirt she wore as he pressed kisses onto her breasts. Her hands clasped behind his head. Her fingers entwined in the lushness of his hair. She held his mouth to her breast. Needing him. Wanting him.

"I want you," he whispered huskily. "Here, now."

"I want you too," she responded eagerly.

He pulled, half carried her to a cane sofa on the far side of the veranda. The hardness of the cane pressed into her back; she heard his soft murmurings of promises of love to come and lost herself in the magic of the night, the stars, and Will.

Feeling the coolness of his hand on her skin, she wanted this man with a passion and desire that scared her.

A back screen door slammed on the other side of the house and its echo swung her back into reality.

She sat up, stuffing her shirt into her jean top. "I think we need coffee." What was she doing? Isn't this what she wanted? Will making love with her?

What was she so scared of?

Oh, she'd fallen into the pit of temptation once and once only. There was no way she would ever allow Will to make love to her ever again. My God, she'd end up without a mind of her own, kissing his boots and dribbling over his shirt. She'd become his yes woman. And that's exactly what the gorgeous but oh so dangerous William Knight wanted.

Wrong girl, Will. Too shrewd, Will. Too on the ball, Will.

Her self-talk restored her spirit. She could handle this situation standing on her head. She may love Will Knight deeply but she could resist his attempts to make love to her. Let Will throw cupid arrows her way, she was wearing her steel reinforced underwear.

She looked up at his face, mute and unreadable. What was Will thinking? What were his feelings? Did he even like her? How could she tell?

The sad part of it all was she would never know if Will ever really loved her.

She didn't know if she could live with that.

Chapter Fourteen

A dowry or trousseau is the money, goods, or estate that a woman brings to a marriage—it contrasts with bride price, which is paid by the groom to the bride's parents. Dowry is an ancient custom, and its existence may well predate records of it.

Charli padded barefoot into the bathroom and filled the bath, throwing in scented salts. She tucked her hair into a shower cap not wanting the steaming water to curl her hair any tighter than its natural curl. She creamed her face while waiting for the bath to fill. She painted her fingernails and toenails with a pale pink nail gloss.

Slipping out of her bathrobe, she stepped into the hot water.

The last few weeks had been a whirlwind. Shopping with Ester for her wedding outfit. Meeting his family and friends on a more intimate basis, like lunch or dinner or drinks at the golf club.

Charli didn't fail to notice the raised eyebrows at the haste of their marriage. She didn't care. She was past caring. Let them think how they wished.

It was the same at work. The quiet acceptance at the beginning was stunned silence and now the gossipmongers were at work and talk spread through the office like wildfire. The story she liked the best, and she'd heard this from Judy, was that she'd had an affair with Malcolm Knight, and was pregnant with his love child. Will was marrying her out of duty and to help raise the next heir to Knight Books.

Well, they were nearly correct.

Grabbing the curved edge of the bath with both hands, Charli hoisted herself out of the bath. She wrapped herself in her bathrobe and headed for the bedroom.

Dropping the robe to the floor, she looked objectively at herself in the mirror. She had a nice body, well-proportioned, not voluptuous but pleasantly rounded. She turned to the side and examined the bump. The tiniest protrusion and a thrill of love and excitement filled her. Will's baby.

She donned a tracksuit and padded barefoot to the window, gazing out across the lawn. It was a cool, green, beautiful day.

Her wedding day.

They were to be married at Newman's Chapel in the grounds of Melbourne University where Will had attained his Master of Business Administration and Economics, and afterwards their reception was to be held at Mrs. Knight's home.

There was a light rap on the door.

"Come in, Dad," she called. "I'm decent."

"It's time to get ready. You look like you're dressed for the Winter Olympics."

He sat on her bedroom chair; she laid out satin underwear and mist-fine stockings.

"Are you all right?"

"Sure," she assured him. "Just premarital nerves jangling around like a tambourine with a few metal jingles missing."

"Only natural. I'm on a high myself. Don't want to trip down the aisle or get a coughing fit or something like that. I want it all to go well."

"You'll be great, Dad," she reassured him. "The belle of the ball."

He chuckled. "More like the wallflower."

He was excited about her wedding and had helped her decorate the chapel that morning with delicate pew ornaments combining roses with feathery fern and baby's breath.

"I just wish—" Their gaze connected. "If only mum were here."

He nodded. "She'd've liked Will as much as I do," he said, and heat rushed into her cheeks. "She'd be so proud of you, love. Just like I am. I want to say something now on your special day. I want to say how proud I am of you and what you've accomplished in your life. You're sweet and nice and you think of the other person, and are always there to lend a helping hand.

"From the time you were born you've only ever given Mum and me love and pride."

"Dad," she said. "I've never heard you speak like this before."

"I just wanted you to know, that's all."

She wrapped her arms around his neck, and laid her head on his shoulder. He patted her back. "Thanks, Dad."

If her father knew why she was marrying Will Knight he'd be aghast. He wouldn't understand. She could tell him that she loved Will with all her heart, and would, in truth, be the best wife she could be.

"Would you like a cup of tea or coffee?"

"No thanks, Dad."

"Get a move on; you don't want to be late."

She gave a small humorless laugh. "It's traditional for the bride to be late," she said.

"Yes, but not too late." He gave her a kiss on her cheek. "I'll give you one hour, then I'm coming for you ready or not, Charli girl."

He'd always called her Charli girl before her mother died. Calling her by that special name now made her heart ache. "Oh, Dad," she whispered.

He drew her into his arms and it was the first time he had shown her any genuine affection since her mother's death.

"Hush, hush," he said. "I know how hard it's been for you over the years since your mum passed away. I've neglected you. I realize that now. I was selfish and wrapped up in my own grief. I wanted to be with your mum so I shunned you, and I'm ashamed."

"Oh, Dad I—"

"Let me finish," he insisted. "I love you, Charli girl, and if I let you down, then I'm sorry, but things will be different from now on. I'm your old dad again and about time too, I reckon."

She gave him a hug and kissed him warmly on the cheek. "I love you, Dad."

He moved away from her and when he spoke his voice was husky with emotion. "I'll be back in an hour, so be ready."

True to his word, in one hour there was a rap on the door and her father's voice calling. "Hey, how's it going in there? Are you nearly ready?"

Charli opened the door and her father's breath caught in his throat. "Charli girl, you're beautiful." His voice broke. "If your mother could see you now, how proud she'd be. Will's a lucky man."

Charli wore a bridal dress with a shimmering bodice made from imported silver fabric. Layers and layers of organza made up the skirt, which was detailed with pearls and diamantes. Her hair tightly curled around her face and fastened in the side of her hair, just above her ear, was a small white rose. Her bridal bouquet was white roses, baby's breath, tiny white daisies, and fern tied into a pretty country bunch finished with a white satin bow.

She kissed her father's cheek. "Thanks for the flowers, Dad, they're beautiful."

"You put them to shame," he told her. "You'll come and visit me after you're married. You won't forget your old man, will you?"

She was surprised at his question. "Whatever makes you think that? Why wouldn't we come and visit you?"

"I don't know. You could get caught up in your publishing business. Rushing here, going there. You may change. Money has a way of making people change even if they don't think they could. It sort of happens without you knowing it."

"How could I stop loving you? That would be impossible. It wouldn't matter if I were rich or poor, nothing could alter the way I feel about you; nothing," she stressed.

He gave her a hug. "I'm getting sentimental in my old age. Don't take any notice of the ramblings of your old dad."

They made their way down the stairs and into the waiting car to take them to the church.

"You'll have to visit us, Dad."

"No way," he said shaking his head. "I hate the city."

"You're a snob, Dad," she chided him.

"How do you reckon that out?"

"You tell me not to change and to come and visit you in Rich River, but you won't come and visit us. Think you're too good for us, hey?"

He chortled. "You got me, Charli girl. Nothing can stop me from coming now." He peered out of the window. "Here we are. Good Lord, look at the crowd, it looks like sale day at the market."

She peered over his shoulder. There were people everywhere. Men with still cameras and some with video cameras, and in the midst of it all looking like a clone of the Queen was Ester Knight, dressed in blue lace and wearing a large brimmed blue organdy hat, busily organizing some of Will's university mates to form a guard of honor.

"That's some woman," Steve said.

"Dad, have you got the hots for Ester?" She was going to chastise him when she remembered how long he'd been on his own, and that her father was only fifty. Still young in anyone's book.

"I was just admiring her, that's all. Can't a bloke do that without an inquisition?"

She kissed her cheek. "Of course you can, and it's nice that you like her. She might even like you."

"Now wouldn't that be interesting."

*

Her marriage to Will was a blur to Charli.

She recollected the wedding march beginning and slowly walking down the aisle on her father's arm. She recalled standing in front of the altar and Will's hand taking hers. And she could bring to mind the minister's words when he quoted the Song of Solomon.

Place me like a seal over your heart, like a seal on your arm; for love is as strong as death, its jealousy unyielding as the grave.

It burns like blazing fire, like a mighty flame.

Many waters cannot quench love; rivers cannot wash it away.

If one were to give all the wealth of his house for love, it would be utterly scorned.

She still could feel the coolness of Will's ring on her finger. But most of all she remembered Will's kiss upon her mouth.

The wedding may have been a blur but the reception was more than real. The reception party was held at his mother's home and she'd gone to pains to get the setting as exquisite and expensive looking as possible.

Charli became aware of her surroundings. The sound of laughter, the tinkling of glass and cutlery, and the soft notes of the band playing mood music somewhere in the background.

Michael Meadows, a cousin of Will's, was the Master of Ceremonies. He stood, rather awkwardly, coughed to clear his throat, and then in a booming voice that jarred her ears, said, "Ladies and gentlemen, I give you the bride and groom." He raised his glass toward them. The rest of the wedding party rose to their feet and raised their glasses. "Charli and Will." The band broke into the chorus of "Crazy." Charli thought it most appropriate. That's what they both were, crazy out of their minds.

"Our cue I believe." He took her hand, led her to the center of the room, and dreamingly spun her around the room to a cacophony of applause by their guests.

Charli glanced to her left and was pleasantly surprised to see her father dancing with Ester Knight. Her father was actually flirting with Will's mother. Charli silently gave her approval. Anything that would bring her father back into the world of the living was all right with her, and if it took Ester Knight to do it; then so be it.

"Hey, I seem to be losing you." And he pressed her neatly into his body.

When this was over she'd be alone with him. What would they talk about? What would he do? Would they make love? Her body reacted at the thought and she wondered if Will sensed it.

"Anything wrong?"

"Wrong? No, of course not," she whispered, but was relieved when the dance was over and they were back at their wedding table and Will became occupied with a guest.

How she got through the rest of the preliminaries was a mystery to her. After the wedding breakfast was over, the cake cut and the champagne drunk, she made her excuses and left to change out of her wedding outfit. Although they were not leaving until all the guests had left, she didn't want to remain in her wedding dress for the entire afternoon.

She returned a half an hour later, refreshed and feeling a lot calmer. The lime green dress knit from Peruvian alpaca yarn was perfect. She'd worn the pearls Will had given her with her wedding dress, and now she chose to wear a sacred Inca Tumi, believed to protect the wearer from negative forces and possess the power of eternal love. Judy had given it to her for a special wedding gift.

Will rose to greet her as she slipped into the seat beside him. He leaned over and kissed her cheek. "You smell great," he whispered.

"Thank the intrigue of Mystere de Rochas. As it says on the box, 'a fragrance of depth and mystery.'"

"My thanks to the manufacturers," he said and pushed a small red box toward her. "And my wedding gift to you."

She was truly amazed. "Gift! But Will, I never got you one."

He shrugged his shoulders. "Merely for the sake of the audience," he said, flinging his hand out carelessly toward their guests. "One must keep up the correct protocol." Oddly crestfallen, she managed an ineffectual smile.

She opened the small box and gave a tiny gasp. Nestled inside the crushed velvet was a pair of diamond earrings. "Oh, Will, they're beautiful. Thank you." She removed the pearl earrings she was wearing and fastened in his gift.

"Thought they matched the twinkle in your eyes."

It was a nice thing for him to say, a simple thing, yet it caused her heart to beat frantically in her chest. She was so in love with him. What to do about it? Was there an elixir she could take that would kill off her love for Will? And if there was would she truly swallow it?

*

"Went rather well," he said ushering her into the car.

She didn't answer, but huddled silently in the seat. They'd made the short trip to his home. He drew the car to a halt under the carport. They got out of the car and she preceded him to the front door.

She gave a small gasp as he swept her into his arms. "The traditional wedding needs to be followed through by the traditional carrying over the threshold."

"Put me down, Will."

"Not until we're inside."

He kicked the door shut with the heel of his shoe and placed her on her feet.

He moved into the living room, and crashed down into a large sofa. "God, I'm bushed. I'll be glad to go to bed." He stared directly into her eyes and her heart thundered. She felt giddy and slightly disorientated.

She moved toward the large window and peered outside. "It's only dusk," she said quietly. "Far too early for bed."

He didn't answer her.

She opened the double glass doors and walked out onto a large balcony. Noticing stairs on the left side of the balcony she called back to him. "Where do these stairs lead?"

"To a rooftop garden and swimming pool," he called back. "I'll show you tomorrow."

She leaned her hands on the rail of the balcony and stared out at the darkening shapes. The moon was slung down low over the city, its rays shimmering, splitting the sky into two. The witches' moon her father used to say, and, as a child, she'd believed him literally. She'd stared and stared at the moon and the harder she'd look, the more she could make out the figure of a witch crouched upon a broom.

A chill passed through her. She shivered, wrapping her arms around her chest.

Suddenly he touched her shoulder and she jumped nervously. "Hey, it's only me. Would you like a drink?"

She nodded. "That'd be great."

A drink, a drink, my kingdom for a drink, the words raced stupidly through her mind. Ease up Charli girl, you're running the wild road here. Take a drink, calm down, and relax.

"Champagne?"

"No, not champagne. I'd like a tomato juice."

"The baby?"

"Alcohol's a no-no. I had a sip of champagne at the wedding to keep our secret about the baby."

He returned and handed her a drink. She sipped the icy liquid, grateful for its cooling effect on her suddenly parched throat.

"It's a lovely house," she said.

"Yes," he agreed. "I like it very much. I thought at first I'd modernize it, but now I think that would be a pity."

"Oh, don't change anything, Will. It's perfect."

He bowed his dark head. "Your word is my command."

He took a step closer. Her heart beat so painfully. "The colors are so restful."

"The colors?"

She pointed toward the interior of the room and his gaze followed her pointing finger. "Iris blue and lemon."

"Oh. Yeah, I suppose they are restful."

He moved in a step closer. She moved two away from him.

"It must be hard to keep clean."

His head jerked back slightly. "Excuse me?"

"The sofa, being lemon, keeping it clean I mean, it must be difficult, I should think." Oh God, she was rambling. "Still I expect you have extra special detergents, or some such thing."

"I have a housekeeper, a Mrs. Plunkett, who comes in four days a week, a more than capable woman." He peered down at her. "You're not one of those women who want to do her own housework, are you?"

"Heck no. Housework and me are enemies from way back. It'll be great never having to clean and polish anymore."

"You've got better things to do with your time."

It wasn't what he said, it was the way he said it. He moved in closer. Charli looked nervously left and then right. There wasn't much room for her to move. He was enclosing her into a trap... his trap. If you make love with him, you're doomed. Be strong. Be vigilant.

He bent his head. Her eyes crossed as his mouth came closer and closer. Blinking, she raised her glass and drained it. She thrust the glass toward him, forcing him to pull back from her.

"Care for another?" he said.

She was flooded with relief, albeit temporary, that he would be leaving her, giving her time to regain some sort of composure. "Yes, please."

She took several deep breaths of the cool night air. The suddenly black night sky shone the moon a brilliant orange. A million stars were cobwebbed across the sky from the tip of the moon to the beginning of the world. Somewhere in the background she heard the soft strum of guitars and a fragrance, not unlike jasmine, enveloped her. Her senses reeled and she put out her hand to steady herself.

Pull yourself together, Charli girl, you're a grown woman. And you can bet your last cent that Will arranged this whole kit and caboodle.

"Enjoying the view?" his voice was soft and soothing. It lulled her.

She took the proffered drink. "Yes."

"It's getting cold. Wouldn't you rather come inside?"

"No, it's not cold. I mean the night's cold, but I'm not cold, because I'm warm you see." *Idiot, you idiot, it's the middle of winter, for God's sake.* And she was doing it again, babbling like a brook. Don't lose control of the situation. Keep ahold of your senses. But she was so darn nervous.

He removed the glass from her trembling hand. "Well I'm cold, so please me by coming inside." He placed the glasses on a small cane table, placed his hand around her waist and steered her inside.

She walked to the corner of the room; picked up a magazine and pretended to browse through it. The words were a blurred mess.

"Planning on gardening?"

"What?"

"You're reading Earth Garden. Are you a greenie?"

She flung the magazine to the floor. "I was simply browsing through," she said.

"Do you want to change?"

"Yes." She was so dreadfully shy. Completely unsure of what to do or say.

"Have a shower." He was practically ordering her, and she felt powerless to prevent him from doing so.

"I'd like first to see where I'm sleeping."

He grinned. She likened it to a pit bull terrier gnawing through your leg. "You'll be sleeping with me."

"Oh no, that's where you're wrong. We had an agreement. Each to his own. I insist on my own room."

A flash of annoyance. "We're married."

"And that's enough for any mortal woman to contend with."

"That's fine by me," he said as he preceded her out of the living room and up the stairs. "This is my room. You can take any of the others."

"I'll take this one," she said, indicating the one next to his. Why hadn't she worked out the sleeping arrangements before the wedding? And why was she so disappointed that he hadn't argued with her?

He grunted. Walked into his bedroom. Returned carrying her suitcases. He placed them near the bed. "Everything to your satisfaction?"

"Perfect."

He touched her hair. She drew back. "Rice," he explained.

"Oh."

He ran his finger across her bottom lip. "Wedding cake."

"Wedding cake?"

He kissed her mouth. "Impulse," he said.

"I always go with an impulse."

He kissed her brow, her eyes, her cheek, down to nuzzle her neck. She held her breath. He unbuttoned the back of her dress. "Like to help anyway I can."

"I always need help."

Her dress pooled around her feet. He pulled her into him, his fingers fumbling with the hooks of her bra. She stood before him clad only in her brief lace panties. He touched the sacred Inca Tumi? "Lovely," he said.

"It protects the wearer from negative forces and possesses the power of eternal love."

"Is it working?"

"I don't know."

He traced the outline of the necklace with his fingertip. Trailing down her belly, circling her navel and threading his fingers beneath the elastic of her panties. His hand ran over the smoothness of her hipline. She shivered.

He stood back and admiration flashed into his eyes. She was wonderfully alive, and past caring what was right or wrong. She wanted Will. She trembled as he ran his hands lightly over her breasts. Her nipples tightened. A zigzag of pleasure speared the nub of her.

"Undress me," he said softly.

With trembling fingers, she slipped his coat from his shoulders. His tie and shirt followed. Sweet seduction filled her as she slipped the belt from his slacks.

He was naked and he was more magnificent than she remembered.

He was broad of shoulder and slim hips. His skin was evenly tanned and the muscles rippled with each move he made. It was obvious he worked out, the sinewy muscles in his arms and chest were testament to that.

Her eyes traveled down his chest to his fascinating naval, to the thick thatch of hair trailing down to his penis. My God, this man lacked nothing.

She closed her eyes tightly but the image of him danced before her eyes. Her eyes flew open. He had his back to her placing his watch on the bureau. His sculpted back. The deep indentation of his spine. The manly curve of his hips and the tightness of his backside excited her. She ached to run her hands over the smoothness of his skin.

Furiously her heart thumped. Her blood pressure rose as desire swept through her. She stirred. Her sex throbbed. Whatever else Will was, he was desirable.

He turned and smiled. Her heart melted. "Take your panties off for me."

She wiggled out of her underwear, kicking them away with her foot.

With one easy movement, he lifted her into his arms and placed her on the bed. He kissed her hair, her brow, her eyelids, the tip of her nose and finally her waiting mouth.

His hand pressed her breast. Her arm wrapped around his neck as she brought his mouth down. He suckled her.

His mouth left her breast and claimed hers in a wild and passionate kiss. He loomed over her. His dark head bowed. Where his mouth touched, electricity burned.

He found the essence of her.

A myriad of sensations flooded her. The sweet anticipating thrill in her groin.

Her body rocked.

Her heart thundered.

More alive than she'd ever been.

He lowered himself upon her. She welcomed the sensual weight of him. They rotated their bodies. She wrapped her legs around his hips. Clasped her arms around his shoulders. He buried his head in the cradle of her neck.

"I love you," she said as he entered her.

His hand slid beneath her waist as he dove deeper inside her.

He grunted as they went into rhythm.

She held him as if she would never release him. Her fingertips pressed into his back, her nails dug into his flesh, and Will groaned as if the pain thrilled him.

"I love you," she repeated in her delirium.

He collapsed on top of her. He'd uttered no words of love or affection.

She placed a trembling hand on his hair. It was damp with perspiration. She stroked his back and shoulders.

She'd never understood what love was all about until now. Never knew what giving meant, until now. Never realized what it was like to love another more than herself, until now...until Will.

She kissed the top of his head. He moaned softly.

He held out his arm and she cradled into him. "We can make a go of this marriage," he said.

Don't say anything. Don't make it mundane. Let me pretend, if only for this night, that you love me.

Fool. Silly fool. And she wished he'd leave her alone so that she could curl up in her misery.

Oh, my God. Had he heard me when I'd said I loved him? Please, no. Don't make me any more vulnerable than I already am with him. Make me as unrelentingly cool as he is toward me. Don't let me show Will how much I love him. How much I want him.

"Yes, I suppose we can."

"Honor and respect, they're the key words. Anything can work if you have honor and respect."

"Hope you're right."

"Yeah, everything's going to be fine."

Charli would never tell Will how much he affected her. How the mere touch of his hand sent her emotions in different directions until she couldn't tell if she was on solid ground or walking on air.

She knew positively that if Will had the remotest idea how she truly felt, he'd tease her unmercifully. The power it would give him would be intolerable. He was arrogant enough now. Whatever happened between them, she had to keep her deep love for Will a secret. He must never learn the truth or her life would be hell.

It didn't matter how he made love to her; the truth would always separate them.

He spun away from her. She could hear his labored breathing, quickly turning into a deep, bordering on snore-like, sound. He was sound asleep, but she could never sleep. She wanted to lie here beside him and wonder at the things he had done to her. She wanted him inside her again. She was insatiable.

She snuggled into his body and he stirred slightly. She buried her face into the warmth of his back and kissed him gently down his spine. She fingered his hair at the base of his neck, wallowing in the thick texture of his hair; the way it curled slightly up at the end. She rang her fingertip across one shoulder and then the other, and his hand came up to brush her away and to scratch where her fingertips had tickled the skin. Her knees came up to curve into his buttocks and she placed an arm around his waist; her body protected, warm, and completely relaxed.

Chapter Fifteen

A Marriage of Convenience, the phrase is a calque of French:
marriage de covenance, is arranged for personal gain.

Charli opened her eyes and looked straight out of the bedroom window into a china-blue sky. It was a glorious day with no hint of rain.

Will.

She spread out her arm; the bed was empty. She sat upright and heard the shower running and, relieved, she lay back among the pillows.

She stretched luxuriously under the warm covers, reluctant to start the day. She glanced at her bedside clock. Would it matter if she didn't get up? If she wanted to, there was nothing to stop her from lying here all day and dreaming.

She laughed softly. What a romantic fool. But if she lay in bed long enough Will would come back and find her eagerly waiting for him.

She flushed. Will now monopolized her.

He entered the bedroom. "Good morning," he said and came and sat on the edge of the bed.

She lowered her eyelids. Wanting to look at him, drink him in, but afraid she wouldn't be able to control her emotions. "Good morning," she replied.

"How about breakfast on the terrace?"

"Sounds good."

"Mrs. Plunkett is preparing it as we speak."

Charli was ravenous as if she hadn't eaten food for days.

He pulled back the covers. "Get ready," he said and playfully spanked her rump as she got out of bed.

She looked at herself in the bathroom mirror. She didn't appear any different and yet somehow she was. She seemed surer of herself, as if an aura of confidence surrounded her. Boldness, more daring. She peered closer at her image. Her skin seemed clearer; her eyes brighter. Throwing her arms high into the air, she did a small pivot. From this moment on her life would become exciting just from the fact of knowing him. He had brought her to heights that she didn't know existed. He had given her a glimpse of paradise and she wanted more.

Stepping into the shower, she stood under the steaming spray of water and, in top voice, broke into a chorus of "Waltzing Matilda."

Dressed in a bathrobe, she joined him on the terrace. He stood. Charli gasped as strong hands spanned her waist. Her breath caught in her throat as he pulled her into him. His lips moved over hers and they kissed, hungrily.

His mouth never left hers as he moved them from the terrace back into the bedroom. He fell beside her on the bed and they made love.

Charli had the delicious thought that he loved her as deeply as she loved him.

*

They had just finished breakfast. Charli gazed out over the city skyline; the day was dull and hazy. She turned her gaze to Will, absorbed in reading the Sunday morning paper. It would be strange working with him now that he was her husband, but not impossible. She was too much the professional to allow their altered relationship to interfere in the efficient running of Knight Books. The company meant too much to both of them.

He spoke to her. "Settling in okay?"

She smiled. "Yes, very much so."

"Good."

"When do you use the hotel room?"

"Mostly when interstate or overseas visitors come."

"Will we take the tram or will we drive?"

His turn to look surprised. "Tram? I don't understand."

"To work."

"There's no need for you to work."

"There's every need in the world," she argued. "I'm chief editor and most importantly, I need to work."

He chewed his bottom lip. "I didn't suppose you'd want to work now that we're married."

She relished the flash of anger. Did he really expect her to sit home and watch soapies on television? "I intend to work, Will. I intend to run Knight Books with you. I intend to make decisions and—"

"You intend?" He threw down the newspaper and stood. Hands on his hips. "What about me? What about what I intend? You know my feelings about working with women."

"Because of your first wife? The way she cheated on you and took away your star writers?"

"Yeah, that's exactly why I want you to stay home where you belong."

"Where I belong? What is this? The eighteenth century? We've had women's lib for a long time now, Will."

She drew in a stabilizing breath. "So you think I might run off. Cheat you. Destroy you as she did?"

He had the grace to look ashamed. "I didn't exactly mean that."

She controlled her temper with effort. "I intend to work for the sake of my sanity."

He chortled. "For a minute there I thought you were going to say for the sake of love."

"I'd rather love a rattlesnake."

"I have no illusions about your feelings for me, but—"

She cut in on him. "And I have none about yours for me, let's keep it that way."

"That's fine with me. Can you tell me what in the hell I'm doing here?"

"Yeah, wasting your time."

"You're my wife and there are certain obligations that go with that privilege and I expect you to uphold each and every one of them."

"You pompous ass. Privilege? My God, just who do you think you are? So I must never blemish the Knight name."

"You're dead right, because you wouldn't like the consequences if you did. Do I make myself clear?"

She didn't answer him.

"Do I make myself clear?" he repeated.

"Abundantly clear," she said. "I hate you." Oh my God, what a childish thing to say to him, but she was so darn mad, so frustrated she could scream.

His eyes glittered. "I can live with that."

"I wish I'd never married you." She so wanted to stir him up, hurt him like he was hurting her. She was being such an idiot. Why didn't she stamp her foot and drop her bottom lip?

"Too bad," he said, his jaw tense, the veins in his neck standing out like rope.

She hated him. She loved him. She hated him. Oh, dear God, she loved him.

She tilted her head and stared defiantly into his eyes, refusing for him to see how his words had hurt her. "I never anticipated love from you. We made a deal and I'll stick to it."

"All the way?"

"All the way."

"That's all I want," he said, and her heart died.

Chapter Sixteen

Marriage is considered a business contract, yet, with time,
many couples fall deeply in love.

On weekends, mostly Charli spent her time in the garden. She'd
never tire of the beauty of the house and surrounds; in an odd
way, she was content with her life, and though contentment was a
long way short of love it was about all she could expect.

Dinner that night was pleasant, except Will was engrossed with
papers he'd brought from the office. "More salad?" she inquired.
He didn't answer. She sighed and tried another tactic. "There's a
grub on your lettuce?"

He looked up at her. "Did you say something?"

"More salad?"

"No, no thanks," he said, looking across at Charli. "I want you
to read this manuscript."

She reached for the proffered sheets, thrilled that he was asking
her opinion. "Do you think it has promise?"

"It looks good."

"What genre?"

"A murder mystery. One of the best I've read for a while. You'll
never guess who dunnit."

"I don't know, I'm a whiz at picking the murderer. Agatha
Christie fan from way back."

He smiled. "Don't read it now—over the weekend will be fine."

"I'm anxious to read it now. I'll start it later in bed."

"Up to you."

"Coffee?"

He stood up and came to her side. "Let's have coffee in the lounge. I'll light a fire and we'll have a brandy." He laughed softly. "I'll have a brandy, you can have a lemonade."

A warm glow spread through her as she followed him into the lounge. She loved this time with him. Just the two of them. Let's play house. All she wanted to complete the perfect picture would be your bed or mine. Don't kid yourself. This was a complete sham. Two people each playing a specific role. Will the perfect loving husband, and she the devoted wife. She wondered how long they could put up the pretense and what would happen when it all tumbled down around them.

How would they pick up the pieces?

Will lit the fire and she sat in an oversized lounge chair. He stood in front of the roaring, open fire, one elbow resting on the mantelpiece. "I'd like to invite our parents next weekend."

"Do you think your mother would want to come?"

"You still don't feel comfortable with her?"

"To the contrary," she lied. "I'll look forward to the weekend."

Unexpectedly, he moved from his place by the fire and came to her side. He reached down and laced his fingers through hers, warm and strong. Pulling her to her feet, his mouth came into contact with hers. Hot and firm. A liquefying rich reaction infused her, drawing her compellingly to him. Her mouth opened under his pressure, and their kiss deepened to a romantic touch of tongues.

She arched to him with a little moan of hunger.

"Want to come to bed?"

He was a sensual man and needed sex; she wanted their marriage to be as normal as possible; besides, her need for him was forever within her and she wasn't strong enough to ignore it.

"Yes."

Chapter Seventeen

A wife's proper role is to love, honor, and obey her husband, as her marriage vows stated. A wife's place in the family hierarchy is secondary to her husband, but far from being considered unimportant, a wife's duties to tend to her husband and properly raise her children are considered crucial cornerstones of social stability by the Victorians. Women seen as falling short of society's expectations are believed to be deserving of harsh criticism.

Mrs. Plunkett had prepared a sumptuous meal for their parents. Seafood chowder followed by roast pork loin, scalloped potatoes, and green salad, and the pièce de résistance—a triple-layer chocolate cream cake. The table was grand; the wine chilled. Perfect.

The biggest surprise came when their parents arrived together. Charli peered outside, one car, her dad's. Her father had picked up Ester Knight. Interesting. Her father on a date with Will's mum? They were so opposite in character, the way they lived, the way they thought, and yet it seemed they were attracted to each other. The farmer and the society woman. Good title for a romance.

She kissed her father's cheek. "Dad, come in, make yourself at home." She kissed Ester's cheek. "Ester, how lovely to see you."

Her dad helped Ester with her coat, fussing around her as if she'd lost a limb or two. And when he curled his arm around Ester's shoulders, Charli knew the truth. They were a couple. They had a thing going on. My God, were they in love? Charli didn't know whether to be pleased or shaken.

"Nice place," her dad said as they followed them into the living room.

"It belonged to my husband's brother, Will's uncle. I've always loved it," Ester explained. "It's been neglected over the last years."

"I don't know," her dad said. "Seems to me it's lived in now, and pretty rightly so."

Thanks, Dad.

"Beer, Steve?" Will asked.

"Please," Steve answered.

"Mum?"

"White wine, thank you, William."

He looked at Charli. "Apple juice?"

"Lovely," she said as she took a seat opposite to where her father sat, very, very close to Ester. Charli thought you couldn't get a playing card between them. She was busting to know what was going on between them but didn't know how to broach the subject. She couldn't come right out and say, hey, are you two dating? She'd have to be patient and wait until they broke the news themselves.

Will handed out the drinks. Her dad took a deep swallow from the can, wiped his mouth with the back of his hand, and said, "We've got news."

Wow, she certainly didn't have to wait long. She knew her dad was going to say something spectacular and braced herself for full impact. "News, Dad?"

Ester giggled like a teenager on her first formal date. Had she heard wrongly? Ester giggling, it didn't gel.

Her father placed his beer on a table, placed his arm around Ester's wide shoulders, squeezed gently, and said, "Shall we tell them, ole girl?"

Ester looked adoringly, yes that's the only word to use, adoringly into Steve's eyes and simpered, "Let's."

"We're getting married."

The liquid spurted from Will's mouth. "Wha—What?" Charli handed him a napkin and he dabbed at the offending splashes. He swallowed noticeably. "What did you say, Steve?"

"I said your mum and me are tying the knot."

Charli was stunned into immobility. "Married," she murmured. He could have said murdered for the shock that was trundling through her. Dating, yes. Having a bit of fun together, why not. But marriage? That was the last thing she'd thought, no, wait, she hadn't thought of that at all.

"Now don't go on, children," Ester said. "You heard correctly. Steven and I are going to be married, and we want you both to be happy for us."

"My God, Mum, I didn't know you knew Steve—um, you know—" He ran a hand around the back of his neck. "Intimately."

"Your mum and me haven't been parted since the wedding," Steve said. "We were attracted on first sight; and we went along with it." He turned and kissed Ester on the mouth. "Didn't we, ole girl?"

"We got to talking about the wedding and the arrangements, when we suddenly went off the track," Ester was saying.

Oh, my God, please don't let her go into the intimate details. Charli took a long swallow of juice.

"Too right," Steve said. "And the next thing we knew we were talking about our lives, how lonely we were and then—I mean it wasn't planned or anything, but then—"

"I get the picture," Will said. "You both fell in love."

Her dad and Will's mum? Charli tried to come to terms with the suddenness of it. The mental pictures that were floating through her head of her dad and Ester coming down the aisle. She didn't know how she truly felt. Pleased or disturbed? It was just so bizarre, that's all.

She glanced at the happy couple, at the way her dad was holding Ester's hand, and it came to her how wonderful it was for both of them. They had found each other and they'd never be lonely or afraid again.

Joy bubbled through her. She jumped from her seat and squashed herself between her dad and Ester. She threaded an arm around both their shoulders. "This is the most wonderful news ever." She kissed Ester on the cheek. "You love my dad, and he loves you." She sent Will the look.

He immediately stood and came over to the settee, forcing himself next to Ester. He kissed his mother on the cheek and said, "I couldn't be happier for you, Mum."

"Are you, dear? Are you truly happy for me?"

He nodded and reaching across took Steve's hand. "Congratulations, Steve. Got anyone planned for best man?"

"Yeah, you, you little bugger."

"And me for Matron of Honor," Charli said.

"I wouldn't have anyone else," Ester said squeezing her hand.

"Do you want me to call you dad?" Will said.

Steve laughed. "We talked about this, me and Ester, and yes, we'd like very much for you kids to call us mum and dad."

Ester took Charli's hand. "Does it sit well with you, dear?"

Charli smiled. "Yes, Mum, it surely does."

Will stood. "Calls for a celebration. I'll get champagne."

"Mum?" Charli said.

"Yes, dear?"

"Do you want me to arrange your wedding? I know a great wedding planner. She planned mine to perfection."

Chapter Eighteen

Women are expected to love one man, however it is accepted for men to have multiple partners in their life. If women do have sexual contact with another man, they are seen as ruined or fallen.

Charli was ten minutes late when she arrived at Belgini's, one of the most fashionable restaurants in Melbourne. Anyone who was anyone wanted to be seen here.

Near the front entrance on a hallstand sat a beautiful ceramic vase filled with tall-stemmed irises. The exterior gave little indication of what to expect. When you entered and moved downstairs via a narrow staircase the restaurant dramatically opened out.

Two beautiful high-ceilinged rooms flowing into one another had a quality of Oriental calm and simplicity. The background details were soft, not intrusive, unadorned windows and double French doors allowed for interesting natural light effects and lead to a delightful eating-out garden.

Ester was already seated at the table. Charli waved as she weaved her way through the tables. She sat opposite Ester who smiled brightly at her. "Charli, I do declare you look more ravishing every time I see you. How do you do it?"

Charli smiled back and gave a slight shrug to her shoulders. "It's Mrs. Plunkett's cooking. Before her I lived on take-outs, now she fills me full of greens."

"Well, whatever she's doing is right." She tapped the menu with a brightly colored fingernail. "I ordered watercress soup, followed by a light Scallop and Prawn with Avocado salad." Ester patted her ample thighs and sighed. "Why I bother to diet I can't imagine. The weight seems to stick to my hips like glue. Do you have to go back to work?"

Charli hesitated. She had a lot of work in front of her. She glanced at Ester. "Not really," she replied.

Ester eyes lit up and it pleased Charli. "Feel like some shopping after lunch?"

Charli nodded and took a sip of water.

"I saw this most divine dress in Eliot's as I whizzed past. It's you, I know it's you, and I insist we go and try it on."

Charli had the absurd image of Ester and her both squeezing into one dress and she smiled.

"How's my son? Don't tell me, I know. As grouchy as always I suppose? Exactly like his father, believe me the trouble I had with that man is beyond telling."

The waiter placed the soup in front of them. As he moved away Ester caught his sleeve. "Where are the rolls, Andre?"

"Coming Madam," he assured her.

Charli made a pretense of eating her watercress soup. She wasn't the least bit hungry and eventually gave up trying.

They chatted about generalities while they waited for their salad. The conversation was pleasant and the atmosphere warm. The waiter placed their salads in front of them.

Charli had a nice feeling toward her soon-to-be mother. "Mum, I'm pregnant." Not Mum, pass the salt, or Mum, can I have one of those rolls. Straight out. Go for the jugular.

Ester had just taken a bite of buttered roll, and crumbs crumbled from the corners of her open mouth. Charli couldn't work out who was the more shocked, Ester for the learning or Charli for the telling.

Ester dropped the bread roll. "Pregnant," she echoed. "Oh, my dear girl, this is too divine. A baby." She patted her hair. "Although I'm far too young to be a grandmother."

"You can develop along with the baby," Charli said drolly.

"Your father will be beside himself. He was just saying the other night how much he was looking forward to being a grandfather."

She dabbed her mouth with a napkin, twisted off a piece of bread roll and placed it in her mouth. "How did William take the news of becoming a daddy? He'll be shouting and hooting to the moon, he'll be so excited and proud."

"He's very excited. We both are."

A warm look passed across the older woman's face. She reached across the table and pressed her hand on top of Charli's "I know we haven't really had time to get to know each other, but I want you to know how much I like you. Oh, I can see by the look on your face that statement surprises you. I admit that I was a little skeptical at first, but only because you were so different from the usual type of woman William took out."

"That's because you love my dad; it's made you mellow toward me."

"No, dear, that's not it at all." Ester picked up her fork and stabbed at a slice of ripe tomato. "I'm so glad you married my son and became my daughter," she said sincerely and a gush of affection raced through Charli.

"Then I take it that you're pleased about the baby?"

"Where is that waiter?" Ester signaled for the dessert menu and Charli waited while Ester studied the menu.

Charli half-rose in her seat. Ester spoke and she settled down. "Do you want mousse?"

"No thanks, Mum."

"Oh dear, neither should I but I'm a weak woman for anything I like." She smiled at the waiter. "Chocolate mousse, Andre, with just a dollop of cream."

"Yes, Mrs. Knight."

"Just a dollop, mind you," she stressed. Then as the waiter turned to leave she tugged his coat. "Andre."

"Yes, Madam?"

"And a dollop of ice-cream as well and some of those divine chocolate sprinkles." She turned back to Charli. "What were we talking about?" she said vaguely. "Oh, yes, the baby. I know this delightful seamstress who makes the most wonderful baby layettes—"

Charli looked around the restaurant. A back of a head. So familiar. She knew who it was; it was Will. Sitting in a corner far out of sight, with a beautiful blonde.

A sick sensation washed through her. She couldn't handle this. She'd never thought him a cheat and a liar.

Then, when Will rose in his chair, leant over the table, and kissed this beautiful woman full on the mouth, Charli's heart died.

Liar. Liar.

He was having an affair. She wasn't enough for him. He'd never be satisfied. Never have enough women to ease his ego.

Of all the things she knew him to be, this wasn't one of them. It dismayed her that Will was such a rat fink. That he cared for nothing in his life but women and sex. How could she have thought she loved him? Slobbering over his discarded dirty clothes as if they were a shrine to his male beauty. Curling up close to him each night breathing him in as if he were her life's elixir.

He'd betrayed her.

She'd start a new life with her baby. Oh, she knew the velvet cords that tied them could never now be severed, that the baby held them together. Will would want to see his child, but as far as their marriage went, that was definitely over.

She stared helplessly at his mother scooping mousse into her mouth, still speaking between mouthfuls. Charli could see Ester's bright red lips moving. Her fingers splaying in the air as she accentuated a point, but she didn't hear a word Ester said. All she heard was the pounding of her heart.

Gullible and in love. A perfect combination for such a beast as William Knight.

How could she still love him?

She looked over at the table just as Will stood and took the woman's hand. Arm in arm they left the restaurant.

Chapter Nineteen

During the era symbolized by the reign of Queen Victoria, women did not have suffrage rights, the right to sue, or the right to own property.

Charli threw clothes into a suitcase. She had to get away. She couldn't face Will again. Tears burned; she blinked and they fell in torrents. A pain not unlike a knife pierced her heart.

When she'd first met Will she hadn't wanted to share her life with him. Now she didn't want to think of what her life would be like without him. He'd awakened a passion so strong it scared her. He was the only man she would love. She'd given him a part of herself she could never take back. The essential intangible part of her that was vital to her very existence, now it belonged to him. Without him, she was an empty shell. He owned her, body and soul.

She rummaged through her lingerie drawers, grabbing underwear at random and tossing them unceremoniously into the suitcase. She knew the man she had married. He was stubborn, yes, and he was determined to have his own way, but he was also sweet, kind, and generous and this was the part of Will she'd fallen in love with. She was wrong. Tragically wrong.

Pull yourself together. You're falling to pieces and it's not a pretty sight. You're not the first woman to fall in love with the wrong man, and you won't be the last.

She sat on her bed and twisted a tissue around her trembling fingers. She didn't care. She would make herself not care. She had her child to think of.

Maybe she'd buy property not far from her father. She would raise her child where the air was fresh and clean, away from his father's empire. Away from the fast lane his father always traveled in.

Ester and her dad had planned to spend six months at each other's homes, that way pleasing both of them.

She'd go to Rich River for a few weeks, until she was feeling better inside herself and could make sane decisions about their future.

She knew Ester and her dad would be stressed and unhappy about her decision to leave Will and most probably wouldn't understand her reasons behind her actions, but they would have to accept her decision.

It wouldn't concern Will unduly. He'd run Knight Books alone, what he'd always wanted, not to work hand-in-glove with any woman. Why, he'd pick up his old life like it had never stopped. Women, dance, and song. The life he craved. The life he so deserved.

Will would be relieved that she'd let him off the hook so easily. Glad he was rid of the encumbrance of an unwanted wife. He only married her for the baby. To give their baby his name and protection.

She covered her face with her hands and sobbed as if her heart was broken, as she truly thought it was.

After a long, sad while, she controlled her sobbing and removing a tissue from the box on her dressing table, she wiped her eyes and blew her nose. She picked up the long black box lying next to the tissues. The pearls he'd given her lay snug and beautiful nestled in their black velvet. They gleamed and shimmered at her. She ran her fingertips lovingly across the perfect beads. If only life could be so perfect. She removed the earrings and twisted off the ring he'd placed on her finger on their wedding day alongside her engagement ring, placing it, with the earrings, on top of the black box where he was sure to notice it.

She grabbed her suitcase and took one long, last look around their bedroom.

She struggled to the garage lugging her suitcase. Opening the boot of her Ford Capri, she silently thanked God she'd insisted on keeping her own car even though Will had wanted to sell it. Something had prevented her from doing so and now she was glad. She wouldn't use one of his vehicles. She'd rather crawl on her hands and knees to Rich River.

Will's car pulled up. Transfixed, she watched him emerge from the car. "Will, what are you doing here?"

"My mother telephoned and told me she thought you weren't well and that you'd acted strangely at lunch. Is anything wrong?"

"Everything's wrong, Will. We're wrong and have been from the start. This hasn't been a marriage, not in the true sense of the word." The words were tumbling from her mouth; she couldn't stop them. "Our marriage is a sham, and has been from the very start."

"You knew what you were getting in to. I never lied."

"Yes, yes, I know I did and I'm not blaming you for that. But I should never have accepted anything less than what I wanted from you."

"What in the hell do you mean?"

"You never courted me, Will, and I wanted a man who loves me. I want violins and soft guitars. I want to be wined and dined."

"That's romantic nonsense. Nobody courts a woman anymore. You've got to get your feet back on the ground, Honey. Life is real and tough. You've got a childish view on love. Throbbing hearts, pink-colored sky, rainbows and love songs."

"If it is not that, then I don't want it," she cried. "I want romance and I want a man who loves me for me alone. Not because he had to marry me. I made a mistake. I'm sorry but now I'm going to rectify it. I'm leaving you, Will, and I'm not coming back.

"I thought we could make a go of this marriage, that somehow, some way we'd find love together but I was wrong. You can't love me, Will. You can't love any woman.

"Honey, I—"

"There's nothing more for us to say to each other."

"Where are you going? What are you planning to—"

"Goodbye, Will." She slid in behind the wheel and reversed the car out of the garage down the long driveway, through the gates and out onto the road leading to the main highway.

*

Charli had been driving for over two hours and was tired and cramped and in desperate need of coffee. Deciding to stretch her cramped muscles, she pulled in at the next road diner.

She slid onto a booth and studied the menu. She wasn't hungry, even though she knew she should eat something, if not for her own sake then for her baby's. She ordered a toasted cheese sandwich and a coffee. Sipping her coffee, she allowed her eyes to roam around the diner. At a table at the far end of the restaurant was a young family. The father rose. His baby let forth such a wail at her father leaving her. With a laugh, the man hoisted his child from her safety chair and swung her high on to his shoulders, the child singing with glee. He looked down at his wife and held out his hand and together they walked from the diner, so closely entwined as to nearly be one.

Tears burned the back of Charli's eyes, envious, as the young family entered their car.

She couldn't control her tears and hastily rose from her seat and rushed to the restroom. Rinsing her wrists, she splashed her face with cold water. *You fool, you stupid fool, tears won't alter anything.*

Suddenly she longed to talk to her dad, hear his voice, and feel the warmth of his arms. She was aching for home. To tell her father she was having a baby, and that Will didn't want her. That the only thing he wanted was sex with as many different women as he could manage.

If nobody else in the world understood, her dad did.

Chapter Twenty

The ideal Victorian woman was pure, chaste, refined, and modest. This ideal was supported by etiquette and manners. The etiquette extended to the pretension of never acknowledging the use of undergarments. The discussion of such a topic, it was feared, would gravitate toward unhealthy attention on anatomical details.

Home at last. She looked at her parents' home. Huge sycamore trees almost touched the clouds and trembled in the soft wind, while the house sat among them, surrounded by various shrubs. The front garden was a mass of color. Miniature roses, daisies, and geraniums grew in abundance with no apparent plan, but as nature intended them to grow. The garden flowed gently downhill, allowing wide steps, incorporated naturally into the lawn. Blue and white delphiniums bordered with catmint made a color link with the steely blue spruce on the left. To the right was the bright yellow-framed glasshouse, a perfect contrast to the blue sky overhead and the timber in the rest of the house. A bright red painted wooden barrel filled with geraniums sat beneath the kitchen window.

She beeped the horn, and the front door opened wide and her father came out. Her sweet, wonderful dad dressed in his old tweed jacket and loose-fitting trousers. His briar pipe forever in his mouth. Her heart swelled with love.

She stepped from the car and stretched her cramped muscles. Her father held out his arms and she raced into them. "Dad," she said huskily.

"Charli girl," he said. "You've come for a visit. What a wonderful surprise."

Charli nearly lost control of her emotions. She buried her face into her father's neck, loving the warmth of him. He smelled of hay and earth, and he smelled good. "It's so good to see you."

She grabbed her father's hand and held on tightly as they strolled up the garden path toward the front door. Home. Everything was the same. Everything was normal and as it should be. For the first time since discovering Will's treachery, she felt she could push him from her mind and somehow begin her life again without him. Without him. Oh, dear God what wicked words.

They entered the house. There was a fire burning in the stove in the kitchen, and through habit, this was where they headed.

He took her suitcase from her and bade her sit in the chair near the fire. She obeyed him, pleased that someone was taking control, and sat with a sigh into the chair.

"You made good time, love?"

"Not bad, Dad, the roads were light and I only made the one stop."

He leaned forward as if to study her more closely. "Are you all right, Charli girl, you look a bit washed out."

"I'm fine, Dad, just the drive."

"Hmm. Where's Will? Why didn't he come with you?"

"He's in the middle of contracts. You know, Dad. I had some spare time so I thought I'd grab the chance to come and visit you."

"I'm glad you did. We can have some long chin wags." He chewed his bottom lip. "Didn't have an argument, did you, love? You know, you and Will. Most newly married couples manage a few good gripes, settling down, feeling the restraints. It takes time to work out the boundaries." He laughed softly. "You've got to mark out your territory and say, this is the line you don't cross. Give each other space and respect each other's opinion. It's not easy."

"Everything's fine. Don't worry, Dad." *Not yet anyway. Not until later when I tell you the truth. Now I just want to feel the comfort of knowing you're around and that I'm home and safe.*

"That's fine." He looked wistful. "Do you think Will might come up for a couple of days? Sort of take you home."

"I'm not sure. Depends on how busy he is. We'll wait and see what happens. Okay, Dad?"

She knew how much her father liked Will and how upset he'd be when she told him the truth, but he had to know because she needed her father's help to get through the lonely, lonely months until her baby was born.

"Cup of tea?"

"Love one." She went to rise out of her seat. "I'll put on the kettle."

He jumped to his feet and gently pushed her back. "No way, Charli girl. I'll make this one and you can make the breakfast. Always hated getting breakfast ready. How does that sound?"

Grateful, she leaned her head back, watching her father prepare their tea. "Sounds great, Dad," she said softly.

Chapter Twenty-One

Women's physical activity was a cause of concern at the highest levels of academic research during the Victorian era. In Canada, physicians debated the appropriateness of women using bicycles.

Charli woke well before first light. She didn't feel that total despair she'd carried with her all yesterday. What was there was a dull ache in the area of her heart. A feeling of desperate loss, and maybe that would never really go away.

She slipped out of bed and pulled on a tracksuit. Creeping down the familiar hallway, she reached the kitchen and the flashlight she knew her father always kept in the top dresser drawer. Grabbing her raincoat, she pulled a woolen beret down around her ears and opened the front door. It was freezing yet exhilarating. There wasn't a sound and dawn was just breaking. She switched on the torch and made her way to the large wicker rocking chair, a favorite of her mother's, and sunk into its protective depth. She flicked off the torch as the sun rose. It never ceased to daunt her, the beauty of a newborn day. Golden crimsons streaked with gray, black, and white making irregular patterns across the sky.

She heard the noises of the animals beginning to stir, making waking up noises at the first glimpse of light. A cock crowed, loud and proud, safe and smug in his domain as sole male.

Her father's black Labrador made his weary way up the porch steps and sunk down with a thud across her feet. She leaned down and scratched behind his ears. "Another day, Bullet," she said, and the dog licked her petting fingers. "Good boy," she said.

She left the porch and wandered down to the stables with Bullet trotting slowly beside her. The horses whinnied as she approached the stables. Pulling open the stable doors, she switched on her torch and made her way down the wide aisle until she came to her mare.

She rubbed the horse's flank. "Hi, Rainbow, there's a good girl," she whispered. "Feel like a ride?"

The horse nuzzled her proffered hand. Reaching for the bridle, Charli opted for bareback. She led the horse from the stable and mounted her. Then with a slight click of her heels to urge the horse, Rainbow took off and sure-footedly they flew over the rough terrain. At first, Bullet endeavored to keep up with his mistress and her horse, but after only a few short bounds, he gave up and walked dejectedly back to wait patiently on the porch for their return.

It was grand the feeling of the cool, soft wind streaming through her hair. The magical sounds of the horse's hooves as they landed safe and sure on the earth below her. She wanted to ride forever. She wanted to ride and ride until exhausted, and both girl and horse would crumble to dust and nothing would worry them again.

Oh, foolish thoughts. Stupid, stupid. What she really needed was time. Time healed all wounds, or so she'd been told.

Charli dug her heels firmly into the horse's flanks. "Go, girl," she said. "Go."

And as the horse flew toward the breaking dawn, Charli wasn't sure if tears or the soft dew of the first light stung her cheeks.

Chapter Twenty-Two

Courtship may include the couple going out together in public.
Courtship may also involve private activities, which usually include
much talking together.

Charli poured her father a cup of tea and asked if he had slept well. Engrossed in the morning newspaper, he responded with a nod, peered at her over his newspaper. "You were up early."

"Did I disturb you, Dad?"

"Nothing disturbs me. I just heard you scratching about on the veranda and wondered what you were up to."

"Not enough for you to get out of bed and check," she joked.

"I was too warm and comfortable and dreaming."

"What about?"

"Ester and me."

"You really love her, don't you, Dad?"

"Too bloody right I do. I'm going to make that woman so darn happy she'll sing for the rest of her life."

Charli laughed. "She's lucky."

"So am I, Charli girl. So am I." He buttered a piece of toast, spreading jam thickly across the crispy slice. "So what were you doing so early in the morning?"

"I took Rainbow for a morning run," she said.

"Still a good horse, that mare."

Charli nodded. "More toast, Dad?"

"No, but another cup of tea would go down well."

She topped his cup.

"You okay, love?"

"Yes, I'm fine."

"I don't think you are. I think it's about you and Will, isn't it? I knew yesterday that something's wrong. I hope you're not doing anything too hasty, love. Will's an all right man in my book and you've done yourself proud marrying him."

"Oh, Dad. You just don't understand."

A look of concern crossed her father's face. "There's something you're not telling me. What don't I understand? What's troubling you? Why have you come home to Rich River without your husband?"

She rubbed her eyes with the back of her hands. "Don't ask me that now, Dad. I just can't answer you at the moment. Give me time, please, give me a little time."

Charli moved to the window. A late winter wind was blowing through the trees. They swayed and bent in its path as if in servitude. Her eyes swept over her father's property, every inch of it so familiar, so sweet to her. The barn with its old corrugated iron roof standing forlornly in the side paddock. The gnarled oak tree with the now-frayed rope swing her father had made for her so many years ago.

Her eyes burned with unshed tears as she endeavored to come to terms with what she had learned about Will.

Chapter Twenty-Three

A gentleman should always walk on the outside
when walking with a lady.

It wasn't as easy telling her dad as she'd imagined it to be. He liked Will so much that it would be difficult for him to understand. Maybe he'd try to talk her around, urging her to go back to Will and try again. That was something she just couldn't do.

She wandered through his small apple orchard. Tiny green embryonic fruit hung in abundance on the trees.

Her father called her name. She turned and waved. She spoke as he approached her. "Dad, can we talk, you and me?"

"I was hoping you'd want to talk. I'm worried about you."

"Oh, Dad." She gave a cry. Not a soft cry but a real, wonderful cry that unleashed some of the hurt bottled up inside her. Six years old again, when she'd scraped her knee and her mother had dabbed her cut with iodine, blowing on the gravel rash to help ease the throbbing and her father had stood tall and silent beside her holding her hand tightly.

"Oh my little girl," he said and wrapped his arms around her.

"Dad, oh, Dad," she sobbed.

"Let it rip, Charli girl. Don't bottle up pain or it will become so bad it'll take hold of you. God gave us the power to cry and I reckon he wants us to every time we get hurt and there isn't any shame to that for man or woman."

She cried as though she would never stop. Her father never said another word, just patted her back and kissed the top of her hair. Eventually the tears subsided.

"I'm having a baby, Dad."

"A baby. Oh, Charli girl, that's wonderful."

"Everything is wrong and so damn awful." She drew in a quivering breath. "Oh, Dad I feel lousy."

"Tell me everything," he said.

Charli told her father about Will. Hesitantly at first, then like it would never stop until she had talked the hurt away. She left nothing out, and she colored nothing. She told her father exactly how it was. How much she loved Will, and what the loss of him was doing to her life.

"I don't know what to do, Dad," she said.

They had reached the porch and sat down on the stoop. Her father picked up a stick and drew swirling patterns in the dirt.

"I think you underestimate the man, and besides, he has a right to defend himself."

"No he doesn't," she said crossly. "He was almost salivating over that blonde, couldn't keep his hands off her."

"That doesn't sound like the Will I know."

She sighed. "I want to hurt him, Dad."

"That's because he's hurt you, love. Only natural we want to strike back, but it won't get you anywhere, only add embarrassment to the hurt."

"You're such an old know-it-all."

"Takes practice."

She looked at her father. "What can I do?"

"Well, if you won't talk it out with Will, give him a chance to defend himself—"

"Dad!"

"As I see it you only have one choice. You stay here in Rich River and, after the baby's born, find yourself a job. You can stay with me until you feel you can manage on your own."

"I thought I'd buy property up around here near you."

"Sounds like a good idea. There's the old Martin place going cheap. Not much property but enough for you to look after. You'll have a lot on your hands, love, raising a baby on your own."

"I've got you and Ester."

"Too bloody right, you do."

She sighed deeply. "I love him so much, Dad."

"I know, I know. Now how about us going inside and see what we can rustle up for lunch. I'm starving," he told her.

"Are you ever anything else?" She grinned. "I suppose I have to prepare lunch."

"I can make ham and cheese sandwiches."

She laughed. "That's about my limit too, Dad."

"I might even slice up a tomato or two. How about that, eh, love?"

"Sounds delicious."

He placed his arm around her shoulders and gave her a gentle hug. "Have I ever told you how lucky we were to get such a wonderful kid as you? I love you, Charli girl."

"I love you too, Dad. Very much." Charli's voice was barely a whisper. And suddenly the pain of yesterday was washed away with the promise of tomorrow. Maybe everything would work out and she could begin a new life with her child?

With her arm wrapped around her dad's waist, she walked with him into their warm, inviting kitchen.

Chapter Twenty-Four

*The ideal silhouette of the time demanded a narrow waist, which
was accomplished by constricting the abdomen with a laced corset.
Physicians turned their attention to the use of corsets and determined
that they caused several medical problems; compression of the thorax,
restricted breathing, organ displacement, poor circulation, and
prolapsed uterus.*

Her dad had gone to Portsea to visit Ester and bring her back to
the farm for a few days. Charli was looking forward to Ester's visit.
She knew her dad would tell Ester all that had happened between
Will and her, and she knew that Ester would be upset. She hoped
eventually she'd understand and accept their separation.

She was feeling so much more relaxed since talking with her
dad. He always had a way of making the terrible seem not so
bad after all. That everything had a purpose. She really couldn't
see the reason behind her meeting and falling in love with Will.
She touched her tummy. Maybe this baby had a reason to be
born. Maybe he would be Prime Minister of Australia, or some
wonderful doctor who could find the cure for cancer or maybe
just an ordinary bloke who'd meet a woman and court her until
she fell in love with him.

She filled the sink with hot water and detergent and began
washing dishes.

Her dad was insisting that she stay with him until after the
baby was born. She'd rather get a place of her own and begin her
life; without Will, her heart cried.

The day was cool and frosty as Charli worked in the kitchen.
She was startled by the sound of violins and guitars playing "I Will
Always Love You."

"What the hey—"

She moved to the kitchen door and looked out. An unbelievable sight of Will, holding a huge bunch of white roses, a massive box of candy under one arm, stood with a man playing a violin and a woman playing a guitar; behind them a table was set with white linen, candlesticks, sparkling crystal glasses and a silver bucket holding a chilling bottle of champagne. There was a waiter clad in black and a chef in a white top hat holding a large wicker basket presumably full of food.

And then, to her utter amazement and delight, Will sang the words of the song, his voice so off-key the sound hurt her ears.

She raced outside to stand in front of him. "Will, oh Will, you sweet adorable idiot."

He laced his hands on his lean hips in a rambunctious stance. A soft wind had blown his black hair into disorder; he hadn't shaved, and his jaw had a faint stubble shadow.

They stared at each other and Charli was losing control of her senses. Her heart beat very fast and hard. She stood still and straight, her eyes locked with his.

"You wanted to be courted. I'm a'courtin'." He shoved the candy and flowers into her arms and gathered them all into his arms and they danced, slowly, seductively. Her heart trembled.

"How did you do it? How did you arrange all of this?"

"I hired a plane."

"You're wonderful."

He grinned. "I'm forced to agree with you."

She saw every line of his skin, every hair of his eyebrows, but most of all she could see the promise in his gaze and in the soft lines of his mouth.

He drew her in closer to him. Tears pressed her throat and behind her eyes. Being in his arms had melted the pain from her heart, and she felt warm again.

He whispered her name, oh, so very softly and suddenly they were a fraction apart.

She couldn't speak. She stood there swallowing back those ridiculous tears. The candy and flowers dropped to the ground. She was heedless of everything except the man she loved.

He took her hand and, at his very touch, all the worries and heartache of the past few days disappeared.

"Could you really say goodbye? Never see me again?"

"Will, oh Will."

"Did you imagine I'd ever let you go? Did you believe I wouldn't come after you?"

Still unsure of him and her own frailty where he was concerned, she spoke harshly. "There are those who love and those who love too much. I'm one of the latter. Please, whatever you do, don't pretend anymore. I can't take it." She turned and raced back inside the house. He followed her.

"Let's go home."

"It's not that simple."

"The hell it isn't."

He had to admit the truth that he didn't really want to be married to her. That he needed other women in his life. Then she could be rid of him and the ghost of him that haunted her day and night and she might find peace and contentment here in Rich River with her father and her child.

"I'm not coming back with you, Will. Don't pretend anymore," she said. "There's no one around to see you play the perfect husband. Admit the truth, Will."

"The truth," he said husky voiced. "You wouldn't know the truth if it hit you fair in the face." He brought her to him. "You stupid little fool. Don't you know? Didn't you ever know? Why did you leave me?"

"Because other women mean more to you than your child?"

"That's a bloody mean thing to say to me." His eyes were as cold as cut glass.

"But true."

"I haven't the foggiest what you're talking about."

"I'm talking about a beautiful blonde, in Belgini's, when I was having lunch with mum."

"Blonde?" he said vaguely.

He drew her to him and this time she didn't resist him. His arms entwined around her waist and they felt good there. The sweet warmth of his breath fanned her face and her heart lost some of its ache.

"Listen to me carefully. That's Stan McPhee's wife."

"Stan McPhee?"

"He's running my publishing house in Darwin. Lauren, that's his wife's name, made a special trip down to Melbourne to talk to me."

"About what?"

"About Stan. It seems Stan has a chance of opening his own business but he won't take the opportunity because he doesn't want to let me down."

"Oh Will."

"I met Lauren at the restaurant and told her I'd fix it so Stan could have his dream."

"What did you do?"

"I fired him." He chuckled. "Boy, was he surprised, and then he knew and thanked me."

"Who'll run the show in Darwin?"

"Me, until I sort things out. Find a suitable person to take over the reins."

"And Knight Books. What will happen there?"

"You, my love, will handle everything while I'm gone. I know you can do it, Honey. You could run Knight Books with one hand tied behind your back."

"Oh, Will, I was so jealous."

"Don't you know? Didn't you ever know? Couldn't you just once, especially when we were making love, sense that I was in love with you?"

"You love me?"

He breathed into her hair. "Honey, you beautiful, impossible, wonderful woman, I was crazy about you from the first moment I saw you."

She entwined her arms around his neck and kissed him gently on the mouth. "Why didn't you tell me, Will? Why did you go on letting me believe you were…"

"Some kind of sex monster?" He kissed her eager mouth. "Only with you. There is not and never will be another woman in my life." He kissed her again. "I want to give you the moon, the sun, the stars. All I have is my heart. It's yours if you want it."

"I want it, I want it. You never told me you loved me, Will. Not once."

"I was afraid you'd throw it back in my face if I bared my soul—my real feelings for you."

"I can't believe this is all happening. That you really love me."

"I love you and I shall never love anyone but you," he told her huskily. "I love you as far as my life shall reach."

Her voice was low and hoarse. "I love you with all my heart."

"I have something that's yours," he said, and reaching into his hip pocket, he withdrew her wedding ring and placed it back in its rightful place. He bent his head and kissed the finger where his ring lay.

"I'll never take it off again," she whispered.

He slipped his arm around her and bent his head down until his lips met hers in a kiss of unutterable sweetness. A wave of tenderness and love swept over her.

The pressure of his mouth increased on hers. The hand on her cheek slid down to grasp her own eager hand.

Suddenly the world was a wonderfully warm place. In the background she could hear the birds singing, the swish of the trees as they bent and swayed toward the winding river.

And love was hers for eternity.

Notice in *Rich River Gazette*

On May 1st, to Charli and William Knight, a son, Michael William, weighing in at seven pounds, eight ounces. Family deliriously happy. Daddy still a little shaken.

About the Author

Iris Leach lives with her husband Michael in Wandin in the Yarra Valley, a small community around 50 kilometeres from Melbourne, where grapes are grown and made into delicious wine. She likes talking with her friends, movies, knitting, and reading romance.

In the mood for more Crimson Romance? Check out *The Spanish Acquisition* by Nora Snowdon at *CrimsonRomance.com*.

www.ingramcontent.com/pod-product-compliance
Lightning Source LLC
Chambersburg PA
CBHW010642100726
47900CB00011B/2933